SONG OF THE NIGHT

ZOE BURGESS

Britain's Next
BESTSELLER

For my late father who taught me to never give up on my passions

Contents

Prologue

Burning Sun

I CALL IT LUST, OR OBSESSION.

I'm too old to remember the meaning of love, of how it really feels. This obsession is the closest I can come.

I know it's real. His image haunts my mind; every curve of his body etched to memory, every sound and motion makes me crave him.

Although, thus far, I have only watched in isolation, not daring to break the spell he has over me. And yes, I know he's male, he may fool all you mortals that watch him, with his angelic voice as he sings and the softness of his step; each taken with such careful grace, never too urgent or rushed, as if every motion is special. He almost glides with elegance, so different from any other man. His gentle face, with its delicate features. Not a blemish, just pure smooth skin. Such a picture of innocence framed with flowing hair, like a curtain of silk. A shade of platinum blonde that sits about him like a sheet of snow. And set into this face, those eyes of crystal blue. So piercing, yet so distant. He looks like winter itself was put into human form. So cold and distant, if anyone got close to him he'd shatter like glass.

But I've watched him in his sleep, the way the sheet clings to his slim form, hair cascading over his pillow. So still. So peaceful. He is much happier in whatever world he goes to when he sleeps.

And so, I come to these operas every night to watch him, ever wondering why he would hide such male beauty behind the façade of a woman. Maybe he thinks his talent would only be appreciated coming from a woman, or only a woman deserves such grace.

If he was male perhaps he would be ridiculed for such beauty. A female façade is safer. A barrier so that no one would get close to him and know his secret. But I know, and it makes no difference to me.

Beauty is beauty.

I feel myself ever drawn to this mortal creature. It saddens me that something so perfect must grow old and die. I have been alone so long, perhaps it's time to take a lover. A bride to soothe my eternal soul.

I want to possess him, hold his form to me; but also care for him, protect him from this world he is hiding from. But such is my love, although I still don't know if this is the right word. Maybe he is the one to teach me what it means to love. It is rare for a mortal to have such a hold on a creature of the night. I cannot bear to just take him. Turn him and make him mine. I want him to come to me, to accept this gift and curse I offer him.

He deserves this choice.

Too long I have watched from afar. Tonight I will go to him. Tonight I will offer immortality and eternal beauty.

It is the greatest gift a man could receive from a being such as myself.

Cold Moon

Another evening passed.

Time seems to move so quickly, yet I still seem not to accomplish anything. I have my fame and an opera house full of fans; but they are here to see the great female singer, not the man beneath. How betrayed would they feel if they knew my secret? I have no choice; my true self caused nothing but pain and grief.

Recently I feel as if I'm being watched. I know it sounds stupid, I'm watched every night. This is different. It feels like someone is watching the real me. Finally away from the people and world I perform in, I stand in front of my dresser. My reflection, or should I say *my façade*, stares back at me.

The roses I received look like blood held against my pale form.

I hate this guise. Not because I hate my appearance, but because I know that I would not be accepted without it. There is no escape. I'm trapped in a body I made for myself, never feeling the appreciation of who I truly am.

My arms loosen, the blood red roses fall at my feet. If only I wasn't such a *weak* person, afraid of what everyone thinks of me. But at least here, in my own home, I can be myself. I peel off the beautiful fabric of the white dress that entwines me. The feel of it when it slides from my body is comforting. I begin to remove my make-up.

It still amazes me how much something like this can hide one's true appearance. But even without it, my skin is still pale and my lips delicate. I love the sensation of getting prepared for a performance just as much as when it's time to remove that part of me. It's a shame no one would understand the comfort I feel. It's fine to wear beautiful clothes if you're a beautiful woman.

But, a beautiful man? That would never be accepted.

My garment discarded, I look at the real me. Even my figure is feminine. I've come to accept that, but people are prejudiced. That's why I'm so distant. No one can hurt me if they don't know me. I can be cold, and uncaring. I don't need emotion. To feel for someone would mean to let them close, and what man would love me when they find out what lies beneath the façade?

I go to bed just as I am, the sheets clinging to my naked form. It's comforting to feel the fabric against me. It reminds me that my body is still male. That you can change the surface with clothes, jewels and make-up, but not your own skin. Underneath it all I am still male.

Bed is a relief. At least in sleep I'm male.

In dreams, I'm free.

As I drift off to a better place, there's that feeling of being watched once more. Eyes that seem to burn into my very soul. It's such a different feeling from being watched in the opera house. It's almost intoxicating. It's not the looks of jealousy from women, or the star struck men in the opera house. It's powerful, and raw. Dangerous. It feels as if great passion is being focused on me.

The me as I am now.

Maybe, just maybe, whoever has this power can be the one to break me out of my cold shell. Maybe I've found something more to life. Something real, that's not just a dream. I hope whoever is out there comes to me soon.

Before I decide that I don't want to wake up.

Chapter 1

Yue-ren

THE MOONS LAMENT

A COLD CHILL BLEW THROUGH THE OPERA HOUSE, making it feel more haunted than usual.

The building stood with such an imposing aura that it still amazed people how popular a venue it was. The walls are black stone with engraved marble pillars and steps. It looks more like a dark temple than a building where performances are given. Inside it has rich red walls and thick curtains. More of the black marble paves the floor, and its high ceiling has deep mahogany beams supporting it.

Even inside it feels oppressive, with its large gold-framed paintings of former opera stars lining the walls, all staring at the people who walk below them into the vast auditorium.

The auditorium itself is a large, round room with red-cushioned seats. Its red walls lit by pockets of light from the many candles scattered around. It is, by far, the most comforting part of the building; it is warm, and here the voices of the audience can be heard, giving the room a friendlier feel. But away from this room are cold corridors, decorated with ornate statues and those haunting paintings whose eyes watch you as you walk by.

It is not a place a child would enjoy growing up in, and yet this is my home as much as it was my mother's when she was alive.

The great talent and beauty, Selena-ren. The most famous opera singer of her time.

My mother.

Many would have loved such a star for a mother, being raised in such a life of luxury. I couldn't really call it 'being raised'. After a while, I realised that I had been nothing more than a fad. Something a woman who had everything could enjoy for a while. At first, she was loving enough, but she soon tired of a child. There were so many other pleasures in life she could console herself with. She was always surrounded by handsome men. So many that, to this day, I never knew which was my father. Nor did she. Her money and fame bought her clothes, make-up, jewellery. Never anything a small child could play with, so her clothes and jewels became my toys. Maybe that's why I still dress like her now. I never had a father figure, so I had to rely on a woman who loved her own appearance more than her child.

I remember her once saying when she thought I wasn't around, how unfortunate it was that I was born male.

If I were a girl, then she would have been able to relate to me, given me everything I would have wanted. Everything she wanted. So I decided, then and there, that I would be a girl. I wore her clothes. Her jewels. I let my hair grow long, and watched what I ate so I could sculpt a more feminine form for myself. It worked well.

Too well, as I found out.

I had everyone treat me as a girl. All my mannerisms were female. I watched my mother move, copying her easy steps and even her singing style, determined to be just like her. I went from school to school, each one realising I was a boy pretending to be a girl. A sick child, they called me. An abomination. A disgrace. My mother, ashamed of my behaviour and not wanting to tarnish her good name by being the mother of such a disturbed child, decided that I would leave school and get my education in the opera house. I was glad to leave school; where the other children would tease, bully, and beat me. Say I was wrong in the head. I was then tutored in all the crafts of a singer and, in a small way, it felt good to learn my mother's craft. I hoped that one day, she would be so pleased that I wanted to be like her. That our shared passion and talent for music would finally bring us close like mother and child should be.

I could never win with her. I didn't understand why it was wrong to want my mother to accept me.

As I grew older, I began to like this new appearance I'd created. I was beautiful, slim, delicate and graceful. I really was my mother's child. By then, my mother had decided that she had never had a son and I was, in fact, a girl. She began to keep my secret. I thought she'd learnt to love me, accept me.

If only she had understood that I had done it all for her so we could be a family.

So she would love me. For a time, all had been fine. She would take me to parties, show me off, let me sing, introduce me to all her male admirers. But, by the age of 15, it had gone sour. Her admirers began to say how beautiful I'd become. How I would be more attractive than my mother, and even my voice had a more unique quality that could make me a bigger star than she. This was when she began to hate me. I was getting more attention. Men would take me to dinner, buy me gifts, request me to sing for them. Some even asked me to marry them.

I loved it; I had fully embraced this new identity. Yet, as I became more popular, my mother became more bitter.

She resented me.

Such was her resentment that she tried to destroy me herself. Ruin her own child for stealing her spotlight, her fans.

She had said that there was a prominent businessman who had come to see me and, if I played my cards right, he would make me a star; just like her. Looking back, it had not been the first time she had used me for her own gain. I had been too naïve to see it, and this encounter was to be our breaking point. Many a time she had introduced me to wealthy men, and I had been too innocent to realise she was trying to prostitute her own child to reclaim her fame and fortune. Luckily, thus far, they had declined such an offer; but the look in some of their eyes had said that they would have accepted if they thought my mother's fall from popularity was worth stopping. But this time, I had not been so lucky. I was introduced to yet another wealthy man, in his late forties.

And I had hated him from the moment I entered the room, for he had licked his lips at the sight of me.

This was one of my mother's entertaining rooms, on the floor just above the auditorium. It was a level of the opera house where there were bars and private chambers, where she hosted her parties. Where guests could sit and talk. Smoking rooms for gentlemen, and elegant halls for the women to sit and discuss those tired old things vain women like to talk about.

This room was smaller.

It was for those one to one meetings, where my mother and her guest could talk in a closer, more comfortable environment.

I had always hated the smell of this room. It smelt of

candles and perfume but underneath it something bitter and adult that my naïve child self found distasteful. If I could place the smell now I would say that it was the smell of vain desire dressed up as adult passion;

Twisted and indulgent, and not at all like the sweet loving emotion I thought it should have smelt like.

My mother left the room. We were alone, and he began to pace around me. I felt as if he was a vulture circling me before he spoke.

"You certainly are as attractive as your mother said you were. Well worth the salvation of her career."

He spoke well but his voice was stained with what I now know as lust, and his eyes were hungry. I soon realised that I was nothing more than prey to him, and it had been my mother who had set the trap.

"Come, my dear. Don't be shy. I'm here to help you, teach you things about the world."

A hand clasped my shoulder, and I tried to pull away. Another caught my face, gripping my chin tightly as he tilted my head so I could accept his kiss. I was so frightened. As a boy of 15, I had never let another man kiss me.

Yes, in my new form I had come to appreciate the good-looking men that flocked around me, but never let them near me.

Never let them touch.

His kiss was violent, forced. Not at all like I had expected my first kiss to be, and I could feel the pressure increase. At last, he broke away from me. I felt sick. Used and frightened, knowing that one kiss would not satisfy him as the hand that had held my chin now began to travel up my leg.

I had to break free. I screamed, kicked and bit until he let go, and I tumbled over the chair landing on the floor. My hair was a mess, my dress crumpled.

Again he reached for my shoulders, pinning me to the floor, yet I would not give up. I pushed myself up, crawled away, but he had hold of my hair, pulling me back.

As I struggled, he ripped the collar of my dress, exposing soft pale flesh.

I will never forget how pleased he looked at seeing my exposed skin as he ripped at my clothing. But, as my upper torso was exposed, he stopped. Relaxed. My mother had neglected to tell this man that I too was male. The confusion flickered in his eyes.

I thought I was safe, my masculinity actually saving me, but I was wrong.

"Well, this is a surprise. But I shouldn't really complain. A beauty like yourself is rare, and your innocence appealing."

His voice dripped with desire. I could feel the tears in my eyes.

I had lost.

This man was stronger than me. There was no escape. My body became limp beneath him as his hand travelled my chest feeling its way lower. For the first time, I wished I had never been born. My life a curse. I was about to have my innocence ripped from me.

I would be disgraced.

I will never really understand what happened next.

It was as if someone had been watching and come to save me. I had resigned myself to my fate and, for the first time, noticed that it was raining outside. In fact, it was quite a storm.

The wind and rain pounding heavily at the window. I caught my own reflection in the glass. I looked so frightened and fragile; my clothes were torn, and I could not tell the difference between the water running its trail down the window and the tears running down my cheek. I looked like I was drowning. The wind causing the glass to tremble slightly, just as I had also begun to shake. I wished the storm raging outside would smash the window, and then maybe my body would crack and break, just like the glass.

Then, as if some great force had pushed its way in, the window shattered. Glass flew into the room, and a violent cold wind swept it at my attacker. In the confusion, I did the only thing I could think of. I ran.

I crawled through the now open window, my already torn clothing catching on fragments of glass that had not been dislodged from the frame. My arms, body and legs were cut and bleeding. By the time I had escaped that room, the bruising on my face and shoulders left by that man began to ache. No matter what the pain, I had to run.

The rain drenched my skin. I couldn't tell if it was rain or tears in my eyes, and the remains of my clothing were sodden and bloodstained, but still, I ran.

———

I never really went into the outside world.

I was not familiar with the streets and buildings that made up the city around the opera house. I had escaped into dark passageways, and all I could hear was the wind whipping down them, like the howl of a wolf.

A wolf which had set its sights on me for its prey.

I was lost and confused. Terrified, and my body felt all the beating the storm was lashing out at me. I felt as ragged and abused as the leaves that had been ripped from the trees. Thrown about, drowned in water and then crushed, only to then be dragged along the ground.

I could not even hear the unevenness of my breath, which I knew was harsh and oppressive. I could hear my heart pound. The sound of it like a warning bell in my ears, beating out a steady rhythm, like that of an executioner's drum. And when I could run no more, when I was thoroughly lost in the unfamiliar and relentless maze, I stopped and looked up into the night sky. Enclosed on each side by the walls of high, imposing buildings, no sign of the end or the beginning of this narrow passageway I had run down.

The sky was just as dark, and the rain fell on me like a midnight shower. A cold and cruel shower, offering neither heat nor comfort. Instead, it provided a flood of fear and isolation, in which I was drowning in. The sky might as well have been spitting poison at me. I thought I had gotten away, but a scared, injured and delicate 15-year-old boy should have known better.

He had caught up with me.

I had managed to run down this dark alley in the hope of finding somewhere to hide, but all was in vain. That look again; I hated it, and his voice was more dangerous, more desperate as he spoke; "Where do you think you're going? I paid good money for you; I would have treated you kindly. Gentle. But if this is where you choose to lose your innocence, then so be it."

I had only made matters worse.

The blow came fast across my face, my head hitting the wall of the alley. I could feel fresh blood as it dripped from the new wound on my forehead, leaving a warm trail in its wake. I tried to use my arms to steady myself on the wall, but he pushed me against it. As much as I screamed in the hope someone would hear, no sound came out.

Even if there were windows further along this building, the harsh weather drowned out any sound I could offer.

His breath was hot against my neck as he dragged me to the ground, and I waited for the inevitable, but it never came. Suddenly, the weight disappeared. I saw the man fly into the wall. He had been ripped from me as if he weighed no more than paper.

I looked up to see my saviour, and in the cold dark of the night, all I could see were amber eyes staring at me, so intense. Never had anyone looked at me like that. The eyes felt dangerous and passionate at the same time.

They bore into me as if they were searching my soul, to see if I had been worth saving.

My saviour turned to my attacker. I could only see his back, but he was definitely male. Tall, with broad shoulders. Such a presence, with golden hair tied in a plait down his back. I wondered why he didn't seem wet at all. Rain didn't cling to him; it looked more like it feared him.

As if the weather itself knew not to embrace the figure standing over my attacker.

Maybe I had hit my head harder than I thought, for it looked as though an invisible force was pushing the vile man into the ground. I could see blood dripping from his nose while his pleas of mercy went unnoticed. It was horrifying. I hated this man for what he would have done to me, but still, I didn't want to see death.

My innocence had been threatened enough, I was not ready to see a man crushed to death in front of me.

"PLEASE STOP!" I called out. My voice came ragged and desperate for air. I hadn't realised I had been holding my breath until that moment, fresh tears in my eyes.

To my amazement, the figure heard my plea; the weather either feared him greatly or respected him enough to calm itself around him so he could hear my strained voice.

"If you touch this child, even go near him again, I will not hold back. Now, out of my sight!"

My saviour had spoken. I had never heard such a voice.

So deep; rich and sensual. I was sure many a woman had fallen for such a voice.

My attacker ran into the night, and I instantly felt safe. My heart raced, and I could feel the blush on my cheeks as the tall figure bent down towards me. He drew his coat around me, then picked me up in strong arms. So warm, I thought. I wanted to talk to him, thank him, and ask him his name. Hear that voice again, but weak from my ordeal, I fell into sleep, despite my desperate efforts to stay awake.

The last thing I heard was that voice, breathing into my ear, "Sleep now. Forget this night and dream."

———

That was the last I heard, or saw, of that man. After our encounter that night, I can't even remember his face. I had woken in my room. The doctors, apparently friends of my mother - as rich and decadent people always think it's a good idea to have a friend who knows medicine - told her that I had been through a lot and she should take better care of me.

She never looked at me again after that day. I was left to do as I pleased. She never once forced her rich friends on me. In fact, she never introduced me to anyone after that night. I watched her career fail, beauty fade, and dependence on alcohol increase.

I continued to sing. It only drove her further into despair, until she could not face existing in the same world as me any longer. She shot herself. But, I think that in a more sober mood she would have shot me, or maybe it was her only true gift to me. A chance to live my own life, out of her shadow.

Either way, I'll never know. I was 16.

I hadn't cried, not even when I saw her body lying in a

pool of blood, or at the funeral. It was strange. She had looked so beautiful that day, just like her former self - before her fall from popularity. It was like a portrait or a perfect statue. Preserving all the grace and beauty she had once held. If she had seen herself, she would have been so happy, looking at how well they had recaptured her natural elegance and beauty.

But she was dead, and what point is there being admired for your looks when you are gone from this world?

I was alone.

My mother was one of the few who knew my secret. Those who did know felt no desire to share it. So, in that sense, I felt relieved; but I had never got what I wanted, and now there was no one left to love or accept me.

Except for a dream and a memory, and a wish I wanted to be fulfilled.

So now, a year later, I'm still here at the opera house. Still under the façade of a woman. Again following in my mother's footsteps. And still waiting to see the man who had saved me two years ago.

———

I am but a shell now, who believes in nothing, especially myself.

And every day I think the same things. I can never express myself; my façade has pushed me so far into myself that only pen and paper know what I am genuinely thinking. Although I have written many letters, there is no one out there to read them, so they stay in their place on my dresser. And as I stare at them now, I write.

These are the pathetic writings of an even more pathetic soul:

Life, hardly, just a waking coma in which time passes

me by. But all the experiences that come with it pass me by as if I don't deserve them. My soul a tortured mess filled with the darkness of hate and lost dreams. Sometimes I wish I could scream out loud, and release this pressure inside of me. But what's the point? No one would hear me. It's too late now. I have become entangled in my own darkness. I could not escape now, even if I tried. If I wanted help, I would not get it. Sometimes I believe I am invisible because no one really sees me. And sometimes I think I cannot speak, as no one will hear me. Some people get depressed and think they are worth nothing, but there is a difference in feeling you are nothing and knowing you are nothing. Sometimes I wish I did not exist, but that would be too easy. I want to be something, but I am never given the chances, or maybe I just don't deserve them. My life is a pointless journey, a void or space that just needs to be filled, but has no real purpose. My friends; do I really have friends? I don't believe so. I am only a convenience. A person who is useful to know. No one really cares about me. They just want to use me to get what they want, and then toss me aside. No one is interested in the real me. The person underneath. The person who is lonely. I am by myself; a person who has friends that treat them like a useful tool is really alone.

I let my pen drop and stare at the paper in front of me.

My true feelings of this life, of this world. I am supposed to be living in an ideal world, created to be every desire and indulgence a human could want. My mother loved what the world had become, but I have no such love; it was all a show, just like me, and yet this indulgent and decadent world has been accepted. It had been hundreds of years since wars destroyed most of the world. Those who survived were the rich, who had the money for protection or to buy their freedom. And when the dust of war had settled, it wasn't the good or righteous left. It wasn't those who fought for a better future. It was those who could afford a future.

The age of the aristocrat had been born.

Those with money re-built the world, and they built it in the images they desired. Those with similar tastes and ambitions had gathered to create their ideal societies using the vast fortunes they had assumed during the ancient conflicts. So what did these wealthy, spoiled survivors do? They created their own personal paradise. Great cities built to recreate their fantasies, and live out lives of indulgence. Technology meant they lived in perfect comfort, so there was no need to work. They had all the time to do what they wanted. Humanity had become selfish and decadent.

Their only pursuits were leisure, entertainment, desire and self-worship.

This opera house is just another place of such human ambition, much like this city.

The new, great London.

Inspired by one of the creator's favourite periods: the Victorian age. Underneath it is run by the latest of technology, but on the surface all the architecture of a period of time so very long ago. The city is a fake, like me; and yet no one cares what matters in this city. In this world. It is what's on the surface. No one cares about the heart and soul, and why should they? Why, with their wealth and beauty, should they want to look into the cold, dark and tortured heart? This place, just like my mother, is all surface value. No real depth, and now even her hollow existence is gone from the world. This place doesn't have anything to connect me to it. No ties, no bonds. I don't exist here, and I don't want to be her replacement.

There is only one wish now, and I am growing so tired

of waiting for it to be granted that I have nearly lost all faith.

A single memory of storm, and fear. A memory of power and anger and a memory of passion and warmth is now corroding, not even having enough strength to hold me together any longer. All hope disappearing into the night like the last breath of the old.

A whisper in the dark that no one can hear.

Chapter 2

Cain

THE SUN'S HUNGER

THE ARISTOCRATS ALWAYS GATHERED HERE.

It was like having my own wine cellar. I'm glad that age has matured my tastes, as well as myself, and I am not rash like my younger brethren who live for the kill rather than the flavour. With age had come wisdom, the wisdom to know my victims, to pick the best of the crop much like a fine wine. It was not about gorging oneself of blood, I no longer have the urge to kill, just to drink and satisfy my tastes to keep up my strength.

Life is more comfortable for me in this aristocratic world, the anger and viciousness of my kind rarely surfaces for I have everything I need within my grasp. Why leave a bloody trail of death behind me so some stupid human law-keeper can hunt me down? No, I knew how to be subtle. This opera house always brought the best meals unlike the trash some of my kind would feed on just to survive. The nightly performances meant it was no effort at all to place myself within their company, and years of life meant I had built an economic status for myself to allow entry to their society. It was in this opera house that it would all begin. My destiny changed so much just because of one small boy.

I had built a reputation for myself, a prominent man of wealth that each night I would appear to leave with someone new. Whether they are male or female, for my purposes, it didn't matter. People had begun to speak about me behind my back; they thought I couldn't hear them. But they would never approach me with their comments on what they really thought of me. It was as if they feared me. In fact, I smelt the fear on them it was as if they all thought I had a hidden secret, that I was dangerous and it was safer to let my conduct continue than to ever approach me. If they only knew how close to the truth they all were. I made sure that I never mixed with the inner circle, the lady of the opera house and her close friends, that would have been a too high profile. I was smart enough to know what company to keep in this place to ensure my true identity and nature was kept hidden.

So tonight after another beautiful performance (and yes, Selena-ren was a fantastic performer, I enjoyed listening to her as much as feeding off her fans), I was doing just that. I don't really see the harm in feeding one's desire. After all, many of these people smoked and drank and it had been my latest victim who had approached me. She was attractive with lightly tanned skin, dark eyes and hair, curls that fell about her face; it was apparent she was of Mediterranean descent. She had come over to me and talked about the performance. Maybe she had not realised my reputation, but that made it easier for me to convince her to leave with me.

Her skin soft, her neck smooth and her blood warm against my lips. This was why the aristocrats tasted so much sweeter. Their blood was as rich as the clothes and jewels they endowed themselves with. Blood that tasted like expensive wine, not stained with cheap liquor, cigarettes or the new drugs many of today's society had chosen to indulge in. And I had my choice, never feeding off someone to the point of death, why should I? There was so much choice, or I could just go back to a previous conquest to taste a choice I had particularly liked. I was living a life of luxury and comfort but something was missing, I was waiting for something or someone.

————

I t was one night in December.

I remember the heavy rain outside, and people had all gathered in the lobby to escape the cold and damp, so I had decided to walk down one of the many passages, not really too bothered by things such as cold. I had often walked the opera house corridors. They were dark and uninhabited. People didn't really want to spend time in cold and haunted halls, but I enjoyed the solitude, the peaceful isolation that these forgotten paths weaved. I could spend my time looking back at the faces of the past, many of which I had seen rise and fall over the years, each taking their first small step onto the stage and then each taking their last deep breath before their bodies no longer held onto life. These hallways, corridors and pathways offered a maze of wonders, hidden rooms and secret stairways. You could get so very lost in this building unless you knew which steps to tread. Of course, I knew every inch of the opera house, I knew it better than the occupants; maids knew their hidden chambers, and secret lodgings and guests knew the grand auditorium, dance hall, bars and those luxurious entertaining rooms, but I knew these still and silent walkways.

They were like a void between two different worlds, and

it was not something you would ever cross, which was why it was a perfect place for me to collect my thoughts and enjoy the luxurious interiors and noble artworks. Here with the faces of the past, I was a part of this building's history, a history I was the only true keeper of, for I had seen so many come and go from this place.

That was when I first saw him. A mere wisp of a boy draped in his mother's clothes and jewels as he ran across the corridor, his eyes so filled with hope. He was most definitely on his way to see someone, and a part of me wished those eyes were looking for me, that he was hoping to meet me. But in a flash he was gone, an image of purity and innocence etched on me forever. He was most definitely the son of Selena; no other child could have crystal blue eyes and white silk hair, and now that I've seen him grow into a man, more beautiful than any creation, that image is still carved into my very being.

Soon after, over the next couple of years, Selena-ren started to introduce her daughter Yue-ren, and although everyone was fooled, I was not.

Yue-ren was the picture of perfection and by 15 was as beautiful as his mother. He sang like an angel, his wisp of a figure had defined into a slender form with graceful movements not losing any of his innocence or purity, but his eyes had begun to look sad. No matter what smile he put on for his admirers or how much he tried to impress his mother, he was treated more like a porcelain figure than a real person. I wanted to protect that innocence but at the same time break him, set him free from his prison.

And so, on that fateful day when that man had tried to rip the very things I treasured in Yue-ren, I made myself known. It was strange how I felt as if something was wrong before I even knew it was. Maybe we had been tied by destiny from the very beginning. I saw the light flicker in that room, saw Yue-ren try to escape his tormenter. The scene had caused me great anger, and that rage itself caused the glass to shatter. For a moment I had been left dazed at the power of my own emotion, did this boy mean more to me than I realised?

When I composed myself, both boy and attacker had fled into the night, so I gave chase following the smell of blood. The blood of an innocent always smelt sweet, like fresh blossom even against the cold rain and muddy streets. So I came upon them in the alley, a frightened boy and an older man full of greed and lust, it was a disgusting sight. I couldn't bear it. This man was about to take what belonged to me. It was then I realised this boy was to haunt my every thought until my obsession grew to love. I ripped the attacker to one side using all my energy to focus on forcing him into the ground. If he could pull such a beautiful creature into the wet, dirty ground, then he should be pushed into it, pushed into the filth he came from. This anger consumed me until I heard his voice ring out, "PLEASE STOP."

I realised then and there that I was about to have the blood of a monster wash over a completely innocent child.

I couldn't taint something I cared so much for. So I let the man limp away, warning him that if he ever tried this again, I would make myself known. As I went to console the source of these new feelings, the anger subsided as new pure emotions swam within me as those eyes once again gleamed with hope, and this time it was directed at me. As I lifted him up, I could see the blush across his face, something I had witnessed on countless victims I had seduced but never before had it looked so beautiful. The red tinted his cheeks as if rose petals had fallen on his very skin, red against alabaster skin. Safely nestled within my coat, I told him to sleep, wishing that he could forget this night so as not to have it stain his innocence and sleep he did within the protection of my arms to dream of better things.

I had left him with a doctor I knew close to his family and watched him as he recovered. I watched his mother abandon him from fear of her own failings and her own self-ishness. I watched as he refused to eat as he wasted away, as beauty was lost, as he kept locked away in his room. He was the embodiment of all the innocence I had lost, all the purity I would never be able to regain after years of living this cursed fate. I held him with more regard than any other human. It was bizarre that my heart could be this open, but I didn't want to see this boy fade, to give up on life, I wanted to see him grow and shine. And so I went to him, watched him as he slept, sweeping long strands of hair from his forehead, wiping the sweat from his brow when he had a nightmare and whispering sweet promises into his ear when he dreamt.

Sometimes I would dare to graze my hand across his face, let it linger on his lips or across his chest to rest above his heart listening to the rhythm as he breathed, watching every rise and fall of his small chest. I would even dare to steal a little kiss, never allowing myself too much, only the lightest of touches as if a feather was brushing over his lips.

His nightmares became so bad that it pained me to watch and I felt guilty at the pleasure I received watching as he thrashed about his bed.

His bedding lay discarded, kicked off the bed through his violent movements, the sheet that remained clung to his skin twisted around him damp with sweat. A thin veil of perspiration coated his skin, and as I leant close I could smell, almost taste, the salty moisture on his skin and how it tempted me. His damp sheets could not hide his figure, his body, he may as well have worn nothing at all I could trace every contour of his body, mapping it. It was like being tested; I could not resist.

It was one of the many reasons I could not stay this close to him, why I had to back away from this body with lips slightly parted as his breath came heavy from dark dreams, his pink lips begged to be kissed. I did what I could, I couldn't hold him, touch him, for fear of waking him or fear of what I might do to him in such a vulnerable state. How I imagined it was I who caused him to sweat to writhe within his bedding, but I had to stay away. I sent him dreams instead, turned nightmares to fantasies so that his dream world would be a haven to escape to, so on some level, prepare him for our eventual meeting where this spell he cast on me would be broken, and I could possess him as he now possesses me.

I never appeared directly to him, I merely made sure that in his dream world I was an unseen presence, something to remind him of why he kept living. I would send him sweet dreams of warmth, safety and love; I'd show him a world where he was a star and loved by many and, most importantly, accepted.

Sometimes when he stood in front of the mirror I would stand behind him admiring the beauty he was becoming, watch him put on or take off the female façade he wore but when he turned or felt my presence, I would just vanish. I realised I was obsessed and this was turning to lust. Too long had I watched so that I could protect his innocence, I now felt I was a threat to it, I had to back away, allow this young man to live without my shadow.

I promised that when the time was right when he was ready to accept me, I would go to him, once he was mature enough to realise what I would eventually offer him.

After his mother passed away, how I longed to go to him to offer comfort and to console him but I could not trust my own desire for him Soon letters began to appear on his desk, things he had written but never sent to anyone. Inwardly I thought they may have been addressed to me, so I read each one. Their contents made it even harder for me to stay as I want so badly to reply to these tales of insecurities.

Dear whoever is listening,

Do you ever feel that although you have friends and family and you know you're loved that you're still alone? I get this all the time, and I don't understand. I think that is my major problem: I don't know who I am, what I am, where I'm going or where I've been. I can't tell what people think of me, who they see or whether what I think and feel is really what I think and feel. I mean, do people see me as aggressive and confident, always having fun, or do they see the shy, depressed person, calling out for friendship? Do they see a dark, haunted person or the person so full of light and energy? Is it even possible to be two different people in one? Which one is the real me, and if they're both parts of me, why are they so different and why can't I help feeling unreal or alone? I believe there are two sides to everyone, different people bring out different qualities, but I can't help but think how so very unlike the parts of me are. It gets so confusing. I'd like to think of myself as beautifully haunting, a combination of both my worlds but I don't know if this is what other people see in me. I have too many thoughts in my head sometimes its hard to see which are real, which are mine, which have been thrust upon me and which I have let in. So please, if you're listening, won't you tell me? I'm too alone and frightened. I can't do this on my own.

Dear, are you still out there,

Do you think that one should keep a friend one doesn't trust? As a friend you don't trust is like a knife in the chest, you feel the pain, but you have two choices. Do you keep it there, letting yourself die slowly as you go numb, losing your emotions, so desperate to have people close to you, you don't mind what they're doing to you? The other choice is, do you end it there, just pull out the knife knowing it will most certainly do more damage killing you more quickly but at least it will be over with no prolonged suffering? I can't tell. All I want is friendship, people to help keep me going. I'm on my own so much, but I'm also tired of the hurt and pain, all this suffering. I don't deserve it. I have open wounds that never heal and scars upon my mind. I've been left too many times, and I've had promises broken too often, maybe I can't trust, and I've lost that part of me. Perhaps if I start crying, will someone notice me? Strong arms to hold me, gentle words to comfort me, that's what a friend should be. No fake promises, no leaving me to die, just there to care for me and help me heal these scars.

To if you even care,

It all came back to me today, the rage, the pain, and the loneliness. The urge to cut myself, to see if I am real. The tears they come, I don't know why but they don't stop. I thought I was falling in love. I'm not sure with what but it was there, but I'm as lonely as ever. I feel anger. It's all come back to me, the way I used to be, tortured, scared, burning and hollow. I see one path for me, I'm doing it alone as it's always meant to be. But I feel that maybe this is how it's supposed to be. My anguish gives me strength and inspiration and if I can't make it in this world, I can in mine. Maybe I like this suffering, my silent thoughts falling on deaf ears, my fading presence in front of clouded eyes. So I should live my life for me, alone, as I owe no one anything and I don't want them anymore anyway.

And on they went like this, and I wish I could go to him.

Instead, I come to the opera every night torturing myself with this vision before me. It made my blood boil and anger surface because I was frustrated with myself. I could feel my true nature, the part of me vicious and savage, wanting some release but I knew I could control it, for I had no other choice. It was one particular night, Yue-ren had sung and how it tempted me so. The opera had been a tragedy, a tale of betrayal and death, Yue-ren's character fighting with emotions and longing unfulfilled that it made her go insane. As I watched Yue-ren, he moved with power and rage, with wildness and un-restraint. I could smell the scent of his sweat, he was perspiring with the weight and movement this role entailed, and the dress he wore, a cream gown petaled with light blue, thick and velvet with sweeping sleeves and bright blue clasps, would wrap about him tightly when he turned or swayed allowing me to trace the curve of his back and the slenderness of his legs.

The final scene, the character had drowned herself, meaning Yue-ren walking into a small tank of water that represented the river. It was like watching milk being poured into water; he was fluid and smooth until his form disappeared beneath the surface and then the deafening crash of applause when he rose again signifying the end of the play. His form was wet, completely sodden, his clothes clung to his body and, even though he was quickly draped with warm towels so as not to chill, it had had enough time to make my mouth dry.

Beautiful white hair like melting snow swept smoothly around his face, small beads of water flowed down his features like soft tears. All the clothing in the world could not have hidden that perfect form enclosed in liquid, his every contour exposed. I had never felt such hunger; I could feel the sharpness of my teeth and glow of my eyes. I wanted to devour the being before me. He was like rich cream, and I was like a cat itching to lap every glorious drop. I had to leave the opera so very quickly after that, I could not hold that vision, it was blinding temptation so deep my blood was like a raging river.

It was harsh and rough, it was twisted and dangerous.

As I was walking to the door, I saw a familiar figure, a familiar face that pushed me even further into dangerous territory.

That man, that vile man from the alley, the one with lust and desire towards what belonged to me, he still came to the opera. How long had he been sneaking about watching my beautiful Yue-ren? From the rush in his steps and quickness of his breaths, he was having ugly and depraved thoughts about the object of my desire. I hated him more then than I ever did before; he was taking pleasure from the sight of what I could barely control myself over. I followed him out into the night, stalked his every step and cursed his every breath until he was within the walls of his home. He lived alone, a modest house with exquisite interiors, had I not been so angry I would have stopped to appreciate the décor as I ghosted through his home. I found him in the bathroom. It was so knowingly perverse, but I knew he would have gone there to pleasure himself on the thoughts of my beautiful snow-capped and winter sheathed love.

It took only the blink of an eye, a fraction of a mortal

second for me to kill him. His head was low, looking at the lust-fuelled work of his hand, the other supporting his plea- sure-ripped body by holding the basin before him. He neither sensed me nor anything else around him during his perverse dance, and when he looked into the mirror with fogged eyes, he didn't see my reflection. My reflection was as much a mystery to the mirror as my presence was to him. I raised my right hand and with all my force drove it into the back of his head, crushing the skull, mirror and wall in one precise, vindictive and fluid motion. His broken body fell to the floor, blood swimming around him, pooling at my feet as well as running down the fractures caused by the impact.

A moment of blind rage, I had caused a death, and I knew that if I did not control my own passions, what kind of ravenous monster would I be to Yue-ren.

I left this house, its only inhabitant dead and forgotten as I walked into the night to find something to refresh my dry throat.

Only the thoughts of Yue-ren and the vision he had been tonight spilt into my mind.

I know that this beautiful man was not only a blessing but now had become my curse, as I have learnt to deal with my true nature to survive as a creature of the night, but I can't seem to survive without this one mortal man. And so I backed away, faded into the night, content to watch from afar so as not to allow this hold he has over me to become a danger to him. But I know I will not be able to restrain forever. Each year he has become more beautiful, and I know that in his heart he is searching for me too.

One day my lust, obsession, desire will all surface, and I will go to him, but when I do, I know within my very soul he will accept me.

Chapter 3

Laphel

THE SHIFTING STORM

IT WAS A WARM NIGHT, THE AIR WAS THICK AND HEAVY with rain clouds about to spill their contents, a storm was most defiantly coming.

How the mood seemed so right for my arrival, bad things always happened in the rain, thunderstorms were like vicious reminders of arising danger. I tried to hide the smirk on my face as I entered the opera house of the performer Selena-ren. All around people chatted flaunting their upper-class backgrounds with conversations of hunting trips, balls and dances. Oh, how dull. I came here to offer my services and get something for myself; I could really bring some interest to this old building and its aristocratic audience.

The current form I held was indeed a handsome human, I had bright green eyes, large and long-lashed, and my face was curtained in black hair, soft as silk. Tall, well built, with a soft tan that only made my eyes that more noticeable, no wonder the ladies of the place looked when I walked past, how amusing females are.

Then I saw her, the object of my desire the one I had

come to devour in all her glory. Selena-ren, tall but not that she stood above her male admirers. Her eyes were of a dusty blue, maybe a hint of grey gave them a haunting appearance and her hair, unlike the other women who kept it up designed in various styles, no, she kept it loose flowing like blankets of snow, so white and pure as she was now. She was beautiful, a rising star of the opera and still so young and innocent, how I was going to enjoy this.

I would offer her all that she was in want of, fame and fortune all she had to do was give herself to me. It would not be difficult to seduce her, and I would take pride in doing so, she is a beauty and should be treated accordingly.

I stalked her through the crowd watching as her admirers flocked to her side lavishing her with gifts and compliments in which she accepted with grace and delicacy.

Her every step was graceful and elegant and her smile sweet and happy, her laugh soft and gentle, ringing out with the same quality she sang with. She seemed so full of joy and hope as people said how she was to be a star she blushed lightly, the faintest tinge of pink on white cheeks. Her fair blush, the way she dipped her head in embarrassment and spoke of how beautiful it would be to be a star. No wonder people loved her, she had a childlike quality in the way she received compliments as if she didn't deserve their praise or was too shy to accept it. She was definitely everything I had hoped for, finally a pure soul and such a beautiful specimen that I could corrupt and manipulate.

My own desire was growing, what would it be like to take the innocence of such a creature, to feel her move beneath me, whisper my name, plead for more and when it overtook her very soul so I could torment her for the rest of her life.

After all, I am what I am, a devourer of innocents, I took great pleasure in ripping apart the very ones I love. I had no desire to give a human my heart; it was far more pleasurable to watch them give up theirs as it was lost to me. I had tasted many humans, so many have already been tainted by their own society. Those who were still innocent were so because no one wanted or needed them. Humans are nothing more than toys for my kind or something to feed off whether it be their flesh, blood or their very soul, they were ours, we who are stronger and superior, they are our playthings. And this woman was to offer the greatest plaything I could have possibly wanted, only she would never realise it.

So I watched her settle on a red sofa, and with the candle lighting, it looked like she was lying in blood, slowly staining her gown as I walked towards her.

"My dear lady, never have I seen such an angel take the time to come before us to sing."

I cringed at the cliché but knew that women of great beauty loved to be told how beautiful they really are. I watched to see the faint blush on her cheeks as she cast her face downwards then politely asked the guests that had accompanied her to leave us to speak.

This was one of her entertaining rooms, a place she would go with her inner circle to discuss whatever vapid things they discussed. It was a huge room, so her guests were able to crowd at the other side without overhearing our conversation. I did have to admire her style though; she was a great fan of dark wood and red.

The interior of this building always looked dark and arousing; with romantic seclusion though this corner seemed to be a room too big to normally feel secluded. This room was no different, the candlelight meant you couldn't really see the walls, which were, in fact, all made of carved wood, I could make out twisting trees with hanging branches. A willow tree at one side swept down to the floor, its branches like a dark river flowing downwards. Amongst these tree motifs, I could see a stag. If I had guessed, this would have been a man's room, maybe the old smoking room for her late father and his friends.

But Selena-ren was smart by replacing all that wooden furniture that would have inhabited this room with a plush sofa which created a beautiful spot for her alone while her guests could talk and mingle, and the candle by her was placed to give her maximum light on her deep red sofa. No one would forget who was the star here. As I spoke, she sipped on a glass of red wine. It looked so violent compared to her complexion, and as a single bead sat on her lip, I leant closer, never breaking eye contact. I took her hand kissed it and with my thumb wiped the bead from her lips, so warm to touch. She smiled and spoke,

"Sir, I do believe that you are quite the ladies' man, but I see your attempt to seduce me. Many have tried, but I'm very particular to who I take to bed. What could you offer me?"

I was slightly taken aback by such confident words from this fair creature, she seemed to have already guessed my intentions, but I would not let that deter me. I whispered in her ear, secretly thankful she was not a dumb beauty, but she had wit and charm, this may be an interesting turn of events. I wanted to see how far her confidence would take her.

"I can offer you everything, dreams will be realised if you let me be your guide."

Slowly I pulled her up to stand; her hand was soft, skin smooth and delicate with the faint hint of lavender lotion. She was smiling at me, the wine glass still in her hand as she began to walk through the crowd letting my hand slip so she could run hers through her hair. I followed, it was quite a turn; she was to seduce me it would seem as she made her exit into the dark corridors of the opera house.

"So sir, you want to show me my dreams, tell me what you offer me." Her voice rang in the darkness of the corridor; I could see her leaning on a wall. Relaxed and confident, not like the childlike presence of before, she was now definitely a woman.

"Don't look so shocked sir, just because I look like an angel, doesn't mean I have to act like one. I'm a woman with desires, and you look like the kind of man who could fulfil them."

Through the darkness I approached her, closer and closer until I could smell her skin as I began to kiss her neck.

"You are a more dangerous woman than you appear, but I'm a more dangerous man. Do you believe in demons?"

I kissed a spot on her neck. As I spoke the words, the wine glass fell from her hand smashing onto the stone floor as she purred from my gentle ministrations.

"So you want me to sell my soul in return for fame and fortune is that it? How about you prove how dangerous you are; I'll let you have my body, then we'll see about my soul."

She was indeed a much darker woman than people knew.

Apparently, she found something in me she wanted, whether or not she believed what I was, she at least saw an equal in her appetite for seduction. She guided me along candlelit corridors, the only sound our footfall on the marble floor. We soon ascended a private staircase; it had been roped off by a think red rope that descended from a velvet curtain. The stairs made of mahogany, the wood carved with leaves and branches. It was ornate and beautiful, yet dark and sinister as if I was being led into a dark forest with its majestic trees and a thick red river of velvet.

This was apparently the staircase that led to her private bedchambers, for the wood of the bannister had the faint smell of lavender hand cream and feminine sweat from all the times she had grazed her hand across the wood.

As we ascended, we came to a heavy door, not a large and imposing door but still made of that same mahogany wood. It surprised me that wood of such standard even existed today, but it proves that money will buy anything and the more you had, the more you spent just to show how wealthy and decadent you were. Selena-ren slipped a gold key out of a spectre pocket hidden within the folds of her dress and unlocked the door.

The room was everything I had expected from Selena-ren, a large bed with purple and lilac sheets made of silk; they were like liquid, a strange liquid of flower petals, gemstones, berries and creams.

The room was all decorated in the rich and beautiful combination. Curtains of deep purple, almost blue, hung by the windows framing the perfect view of the night sky, the chandelier that hung from the ceiling made up of many crystals sparkled and bathed the room in a low clear light. Engraved wooden furniture, everything neat, tidy, perfect. But I was not here to admire her tastes in interior design, no, she was walking towards the bed and as she did the light grew less bright until only the moonlight fell down upon her, making her glow like some ghostly spirit as she unhooked the claps of her dress allowing the moon to worship more of her body.

How many men would have fallen to their knees in the presence of such a sight, a woman that looked like she was the goddess of the moon itself standing before them? And while she looked like the angel of the night, her eyes burned with the lust, of dark passion that any demon would have approved of. It was strange I had come hunting a young woman that in all appearances was an innocent that I would be able to corrupt. In a way I was disappointed; I had come to take the soul of an innocent; instead, I found a woman waiting for such an encounter and even as she beckoned for me to go to her, I was debating if this was really worth it.

But she was indeed beautiful, if only she had been as innocent as she looked. Oh how much I longed for a pure soul to torture, to own.

She drew me onto the bed. I could not deny I wanted her body and a soul was a soul.

I could still have fun, offer her everything she wanted and then take it away. In fact, a plan developed in my mind as I pulled her into an embrace, revelling in her delicious skin. Since she wanted so much to have everything, was so eager to sell herself, I would indeed give her everything, but as punishment for not being able to fulfil my desire, I would take my pleasure in taking it all away and see her wither and fade. Oh how fun it would be to strip her of her beauty, fame and sanity and as I thought of the perfect way to do so, I smiled and began to kiss her passionately. I would enjoy this. I would take this woman's vanities and the very things she enjoys and take them away or turn them against her.

For now, the temptation of the pleasure of the skin would have to satisfy me, and as we made love, I relished in the thought of how wonderful it would be to see her broken.

———

For the remaining years of her life, I was ever present, visiting the opera in different forms but always staying close to her.

She indeed grew in popularity; her fame became well known with her beauty admired by many.

She no longer tried to hide the side of her she showed that fateful night, she now took many lovers, and even I would appear in a form she did not recognise to lie with her again as if to stake my claim. The more I devoured her flesh, the more of her soul she lost, as she grew vain and indulgent. Her passion for drinking, smoke and staining her body with foreign toxins grew, and I delighted to see her body be destroyed by her own desires. Her wealth grew, she lived a life of luxury, had everything she wanted, could afford to poison herself with the most expensive commodities. Her life was complete; she had everything a woman wanted, well almost everything and it was then that he was born.

I had appeared to her as a writer of a magazine.

I wanted an interview with the great sensation Selena-ren. I held the form of a young woman, dull to look at brown eyes and brown hair tied back in a neat ponytail. I wore a simple yet stylish black shirt and a pair of smart black trousers and upon my face lightly framed glasses. In all appearances, I was a learned woman but not from a high-class background of riches. I chose my form to appear no threat to her so that her wealth, beauty and fame would appear to overpower me. I conducted myself like anyone would in an interviewee situation, and my last question was specially chosen.

"So Miss Selena-ren, you have everything a women desires when it comes to material things, but aren't you lonely?"

"My dear girl, I have many to keep me company to comfort me in the night, and I can buy anything I desire to occupy my time, how could I be lonely"?

Although she said it with confidence, there was a hint in

her voice, a curiosity as to what I could possibly think she was missing.

So, of course, I had to enlighten her.

"But you can't buy love or a family, you appear to have no partner, no desire to settle down, have a family, a child to bring up, to teach, to carry on your great name, doesn't that sadden you?"

I had hit the spot; I could see in her eyes that desire to have something more.

"Someone, to carry on my great name? Indeed, what greater thing is there for a woman than to become a mother? Maybe its time to start looking at life a little differently."

And those were her last words to me as I left the opera house and this form.

I had seen it in her eyes; she had no real desire to be a mother, but I knew what she thought. If people saw her as a mother how they would revere her, the great Selena-ren takes time to raise a child, oh how beautiful a mother she would make. Her fans would sing her praises. But I had other plans for this child; I would make sure it was the perfect instrument of Selena-ren's great demise. Selena-ren would forever feel that this child was a curse to her until the day she dies, it would be my ultimate vengeance and a pleasure to see such beauty and talent fall to nothing.

I had to laugh long and hard until I could no longer stand until tears of joy collected at my eyes until my very being shook with joy and anticipation. I, this very creature that I was, a heartless demon, a shapeshifter with as many names as faces, was so full of joy.

For I was Laphiel, creature and consumer of desires and one day the product of this plan will scream out my true name with every fibre of its being.

Chapter 4

THE STAR AMONGST THE DISCARDED

IT WAS A COLD NIGHT, IT ALWAYS SEEMED TO BE THIS pitiful, the sun never seemed to want to shine; it was always dark, emotionless and lonely.

The air was as desolate and lonely as the people who looked upon the dark weather of winter. The streets were abandoned, the people withdrawn and unfriendly, it was the worst place a young girl full of hope and dreams could live, but here I was. Each grey street like a wall in a tin maze, the only colour was that of the rust and decay that had set in. The city always looked so bleak in winter and the harsh times meant that its inhabitants had to struggle harder to survive, that meant moral and emotion was low. In winter people's hearts were as cold as the piercing wind outside.

Morale had been unusually low this winter, more of the old technology had been failing; no one had the kind of money to increase the living standards, and the aristocratic world had turned its back, refusing to acknowledge that any other people apart from them were trying to live in this world.

The heat had gone out in our apartment building, me

being young therefore so full of energy, had to be the one to run to the store for firewood and matches to try and get our boiler back on.

It seems even in this great age technology can fail; well this was a different world to that of the aristocrats, a world where money didn't flow like water, a world they didn't acknowledge. Forgotten people, the working class, the hidden filth denied existence in the great city, all but forgotten and ignored. Now those that had been forgotten tried to live out their lives in cities built with the debris of ancient wars. No fancy rich snob would have wanted to build their ideal cities on the scars of war.

At first, people had tried to move back to the old cities that had not been completely destroyed, but the aristocrats had taken these, pulled them down and used the foundations to build their ideal new towns. Other cities were too polluted by either biological or nuclear weaponry and not fit for humans to live in. What was left were pockets of ground that wars had been fought on and now abandoned. These abandoned deserts were lost and forgotten to the aristocratic world, and this is where small settlements had developed. Machines and debris of a former world had been pulled apart to re-build, but more importantly, the wreckage of the new world had defined these new settlements. In the building of their idealistic civilisations, large machinery and containers for storage and transportation of materials had been used.

When the cities were done the aristocratic no longer needed tankers or storage containers, so these were dumped out into the forgotten planes.

And this is where I reside now, my home, the great dump, a rubbish tip of materials no longer useful or needed by the great human race.

I hated living in a building, well if you call a collection

of metal boxes stacked upon each other a building, full of adults with no one to talk to, but my family was too poor to move, and I had already dropped out of school to work so we could afford to eat. I hated life. I was a dreamer, a romantic, I longed for something or someone, like an angel to come into our lives, hope was all I had now. It began snowing, and the wind picked up, my fingers growing numb as I clenched the package tightly against my chest. I could see my own breath as I panted, breaking into a run; anything to get me home faster. I should have known taking a shortcut was a stupid idea but following the river was faster than trying to navigate through the buildings and their alleys.

The snow was getting heavy, and the path was so little trodden due to harsh conditions it was mostly iced over, but I was cold and miserable, I wanted to be home and warm. I should have slowed down, but I kept my pace, running down the small path, the river running by my side as if we were racing which would get home first, which would reach somewhere warm and safe first. The wind howled in my ears even with my scarf so tight around me my neck felt damp as snowflakes that had fallen on my cheek melted and slid down my throat. I could hear nothing but the wind and river as I sprinted and then I stepped on a patch of black ice, as black as night, as black as the void in my heart from years of growing up in such a desolate place.

I saw the wood rise in the air and tumble down the bank resting in a patch of frozen shrubs. I wish I had been so lucky. In a second I had slipped, and everything went silent. It was like watching something in slow motion I could see myself slip and fall, the water getting close; it was fate I would plummet into the icy wet grave before I had really had a chance to live.

Cold, it was so cold.

I broke the surface spluttering desperately for air trying to swim to make my body listen to me. It was useless. My coat, gloves, shoes and scarf all weighed me down. How ironic that the things that would have protected me from the weather would cause my death now. The water stung me, it bit at me, even my tears were as cold as ice, and my shouts for help could not even form. Desperately I tried to will myself to swim but I was getting tired, my body going numb, my vision blurry, I was getting heavier. It was then I grasped at my last thread of hope, and I saw her, an angel, although I did not know if she was there to take my soul to Heaven or to save me.

My last image before my head fell below the surface and I fell down into the depths was her. She glowed white in the dark; her clothes, skin and hair all the purest form of white, it made the snow look grey in comparison. She was running towards the edge of the river, beautiful silken hair flowing about her and a voice like music rang from her as she dived into the water and then darkness.

Who knows what time it was when I came to, but I felt a weight on me.

As I opened my eyes, I saw a figure draped over me, arm wrapped around me as if they had been trying to pull me up but had also collapsed. In an instant my conscious snapped back into place; the river, the angel and now I was safe on the bank, cold and wet but safe and this person had saved me. I looked at her; she had the palest skin and looked peaceful as she lay there, her beautiful white hair was wet and hung in clumps about her face, her white coat clung to her damp form and was covered in mud from scrambling on the bank.

An angel.

I was in the arms of an angel. I had held onto hope, and I had been saved. As I began to weep I tried to move my body but it was heavy and numb, my voice sounded raspy as I called for help and tried to pull myself into the embrace of my angel.

Minutes passed. I was warmer due to the fact I had another presence against me, and I could hear voices.

"Over here, I see someone, oh god please be ok."

The people began to fuzz out of view, but I clearly saw the face of my father as he picked me up, warming me in a blanket.

"I was saved by an angel, please help her."

Those were my last words as I fell back into sleep.

———

I awoke.

It was daylight; actual sunlight was getting into my room, small beams coming from the cracks in my windows shutters.

I sat up, looked around. It was definitely my home; I had been found and taken home, I was warm and safe but what about my angel? Even the little room I called my own seemed brighter, there was an angel in my house, and it made everything seem more hopeful. I tried to get out of bed, but at the same time, my mother walked in. She must have been up all night, her tired face was paler than normal, and she had dark rings below her eyes and her hair, although still tied back, had a few ashen blond hairs escaping, which was rare for my mother.

But she smiled at me, warm and kind like she always did. She never got angry with me.

"Annabel, my dear Annabel, your father and I are so happy you're okay. If anything had happened… We're so sorry we made you go out in that weather, we should have known better."

I could see the tears form as she spoke. So like my mother to always blame herself; I bet my father was doing the same. My parents were such gentle people, still apologising for the life they had given me but I never let them. I would bring them happiness one day, I would bring them hope like my angel.

"The angel, is she okay? She saved me, oh god please say she's fine."

"Annabel. About that. Your angel is in the other room, but there is something I need to tell you about her. I don't mean to alarm you but…"

Before she could finish her sentence, I was sprinting to the other room.

They must have given her their bedroom, which means she must be hurt. What could have happened? Would God forgive me if I had been the cause of harm to one of his angels? It was only really a few paces; our home was made up of two container units, the top one my bedroom and my parents, a split half way down divided by a metal wall that had once been the side of some vehicle. They said it was half each since my room also had the hole in the floor we used to get between levels, all you did was climb down a rope ladder and you were in a dining room/kitchen, below my parents' room was the bathroom.

I bounded into the room, my father was there, looking worried but smiled as he saw me. He looked like he had had as much sleep as my mother but in his hands I noticed bandages and on the floor, I noticed a small pile also but they were stained with blood.

"What happened? Was she hurt? Please…"

But I couldn't get the words out, and my father crossed the room to me, taking me into his arms as I cried on his chest.

"Everything is fine; your saviour is fine, just sleeping.

The bleeding has stopped. She had a nasty gash on her side; must have used their body to shield you from the debris in the river, but it will heal. There is something you should know about your so-called angel…"

There was a rustling from the bed.

I pulled away slightly from my father as the figure in the bed stirred. I knew that my parents were about to tell me that my angel was human; that's how she managed to bleed but human or not she saved me, she was my angel, and she was beautiful. The figure opened her eyes slowly, a flicker of pain danced in her face until her eyes were fully opened. Oh, I had never seen such eyes crystal blue, so bright, so clear. How could she be human with such features? She got up. My father was saying something about not moving so soon, but she sat up anyway. The sheet around her fell to her waist. I was about to turn, I didn't want her to embarrass herself in front of, but my father still walked over to her side. It was then I noticed that her chest was smooth, pale and smooth, nothing like a woman's and I stared mouth slightly open in shock.

"Annabel, aren't you going to thank the young man? He did save your life."

Male, my angel was male; but how with such eyes framed with long lashes, hair long and silken, skin pure and unblemished and even with the covers about him his form was delicate. I must have been staring hard for he drew the covers about him retreating into the sheets, his head hung with shame and with a couple of simple words spoke.

"I'm glad to see that you're unharmed. Forgive me; it seems I need some rest."

He lay back down on his side, back to us as if he was ashamed to be seen by us.

How guilty I felt.

He had saved me, and I had embarrassed him by staring

at him like an idiot. I just didn't expect someone so beautiful to be male. My father got up, smiled at me and left the room, leaving me with the still form in front of me.

"Thank you for saving me. I'm glad you're okay. Please turn round so I can say thank you to your face. I'm sorry if I made you uncomfortable; I have never seen a man that looked like an angel before."

I must have got through to him for he turned round to me, the pain of movement evident on his face as I felt guilty again for causing him discomfort. But he smiled gently and kindly, like the smile of my mother, yet his face looked so lonely and sad.

"People used to say that about my mother, that she looked like an angel. I never really believed them when they said it to me; it always seemed like they were just replacing her with me, but thank you it's nice that someone honest can give such a compliment."

I blushed. He was charming, beautiful and charming with a delicate voice that matched him so well and yet he seemed fragile.

"Thank you again, but why are you here and not with these people? Sounds like you come from a very different world from me."

"You're smart, what's your name? It would be nice to know who I rescued."

"Annabel! Annabel Montana pleased to meet you."

I held out my hand. I was happy for once, glad to be living in this quiet town where I was able to meet such a person.

"I'm Yue-ren, it's a pleasure."

"Wait, no, it couldn't be. Does that mean your mother is Selena-ren? But I thought you were a girl, what are you doing here? Shouldn't you be living in some great mansion, where it's warm, and there are servants, parties and food?

Why would you ever want to leave such a place? Won't your mother worry? What about your fans? Wait, aren't you meant to be a girl?"

I realised I was babbling; the words just flooding out of my mouth. I couldn't stop, but then I saw that sadness in his face, that sad expression. I had said too much.

"My mother died. I left. I couldn't live her life anymore; I tried but was tired of the façade, I went to look for something or someone."

The last part was barely a whisper; whoever he was looking for must have meant a lot to him, maybe a lover by the silent look of hope in his eyes. It was then I realised what he was saying, I may be a young girl, but I knew all about dreams, about breaking free from a world I was imprisoned in.

"Your mother made everyone believe you were a girl but now she has passed on, you're looking to live life the way you were born, as a man. You want to be more than your mother, background and world chose for you to be. I understand that I want to be more than a poor girl trying to keep her family fed, without using the methods that a girl like myself would use."

In a moment we realised that we trusted each other; hope had been born, and we both knew this encounter was the beginning of better things.

I had someone I thought of as an angel in my life, hope and joy burned in me, and I knew this beauty in front of me would bring hope and comfort to our cold little world. We talked for hours about our lives, our pasts, about everything I could think of. I had been without anyone to talk to, so that it all came pouring out and he listened to every word, never looking away in disgust or judgement. I needed to speak, finally get things out of me that had been bottled up inside for years and it seemed so did he.

Neither of us minded the other one talking; we both listened to each other's stories, both marvelling that we had found someone we were so comfortable to talk to in such a small space of time but then he had saved my life, and that kind of thing really does build a bond between people. I had met someone else like me; someone lonely, afraid, wanting to be more than what people expected of them. I had indeed met a friend, it didn't matter that he wasn't an actual angel; a friend was just as good.

"Then you can stay here, my parents won't mind, you can find a job start a different life with a new family. What do you think?"

"You are definitely a lot smarter than it would appear. I would have to ask your parents, I couldn't impose, but a new life would be wonderful, thank you for understanding. I never thought I'd meet someone like you here."

His words were kind and gentle, it made me laugh how he confused my kindness and happiness as being smart; it wasn't smart to understand him, you didn't need brains to see he was lonely and looking for someone to understand him. He must have lacked so much human compassion in his world, and I wanted to help this man. I left him to rest, running to tell my parents we would have a guest and as I approached the kitchen, I heard them talking.

"The young man is unwell; if we had got there any later, he would have died. He is very undernourished and pale, we have no choice but to let him stay. It will take a while for him to recover properly, I hope we can afford this, but we can't just let him leave. He wouldn't last in this weather, not with his immune system down and with that injury."

My father spoke softly; they were apparently concerned Yue-ren had not been taking care of himself since he left home. He was allowing himself to waste away, maybe even allowing himself to simply give up on life. Perhaps if I found that missing lover I could help find Yue-ren's happiness; he had saved my life now I was going to return the favour. I walked into the kitchen.

"Let Yue-ren stay, I'll work extra hard for this family. He saved me, and he's alone. He can be part of this family, and when he's better, he can help us out. We can't let him wither away, he just needs someone to love and love him back."

I could feel tears again. How many times would I cry today? These tears of sorrow soon turned to tears of joy. My parents were staring at me in shock, but they soon regained composure. Smiling, my mother hugged me, kissing me on my forehead.

"What kind of people would we be if we simply let an angel waste away? God would never forgive us, and we would never forgive ourselves either."

So it was settled; that day we gained another member of our family, acquired a friend.

Even more, Yue-ren was like a brother. I wasn't lonely anymore, and life didn't seem so cold anymore.

Chapter 5

Yue-ren

A SKY FOR THE MOON AND STARS

WHEN I FIRST CAME TO THE CITY I HAD NO IDEA WHAT I would find here, what kind of life I would be walking into.

A year after my mother died I could no longer live amongst those people I had to escape, try and break away from the image she had created for me. A year wasted feeling sorry for myself, hating myself and wishing for something more. I had no one to comfort me, not the real me.

My mother's lies and deceptions had grown so thick that if I suddenly revealed myself if they knew I was male, I would have nowhere to hide. The only comfort came in my sleep from dreams of a distant memory, a faint presence around me just out of touch and sight. Sorrow and depression had set in; this building was even lonelier, all I could see were fakes, people pretending to be there for me, men offering a shoulder to cry on. Well, even I knew what they wished their comfort would bring them and if I had not been living this false life maybe I would have accepted. In truth, there was only one person I wanted comfort from, and he was nothing more than a dream.

All I knew of him were piecing eyes that could see through my façade and a rich voice that could soothe my soul.

So I did the only thing left to do; I left, simple as that.

It had been many years since that encounter in the rain, but out there I knew there was someone who would look at me with passion and desire, no matter what my sex. There was somewhere my façade could end a real life instead of this one where I had let myself wither. The aristocratic world was lonely, but I wasn't sure what kind of world people who couldn't afford such a life of luxury would be like, or if I could find acceptance out there.

The world had grown in such a way that those with power and money gained more control and money building cities for themselves in their favourite designs. The life of an aristocrat meant you could afford to choose what country and time period you lived in. I heard that some of the wealthiest people had built themselves cities reminiscent of ancient Greece, but what about those who had not profited in this new world? I could only speculate about the life out there, but anything was better than living a lie, wasting away from loneliness and despair.

I had travelled for such a long time; the aristocrat's world spread far, and the distance between aristocrat and non-aristocratic cities was immense.

I couldn't tell how far I had gone when I came upon the city of the poor and how I loathed calling it that. It had amazed me due to the vast amount of nothingness that existed in the world. The major cities I knew were connected by great railways that crossed the country, vegetation planted to make the journey seem beautiful. But I did not want to go to another fake city, so I had walk all along them, off into new lands without roads or pathways. The grounds were barren, no vegetation just vast deserts of earth that stretched far across forgotten landscapes.

Every now and then I came across some small uninhabited town that I could have used for shelter but found no people. I had expected to come across the towns faded from memory or poisoned cities, where humans no longer trod but instead just an infinite plane, grey and desolate. Until the landscape changed and became more rugged and hillscapes began to form.

It was then I started to follow the stream as it wound round the new landscape and drop down slowly into a valley. This valley appeared to be a giant rubbish dump with thick smoke rising from it. As I approached this strange world the snow began to fall; it was grey and left a dirty brown slush upon the floor. What a horrid world I had walked into; first grey deserts of lost hope and loneliness, then hills of isolation and a stream running across them like a lost child forgotten and without comfort and now, at last, the first sign of civilisation was a dumping ground framed in grey snow and icy winds that bit at you.

There was no welcoming feeling, it was loss and loneliness, the haunting melody of cold weather and poor conditions and I was going to follow this lonely child of a river and see if I too could be found. All concept of time had passed for me. I had not taken a train, I had simply walked into the night, and the only food was what I bought just before I left the city, which had lasted most of the journey, for I only really picked at it, my appetite not really ever developing. The sun rose and fell, then some days there was so much cloud cover you couldn't tell if time had passed or night had fallen or day had returned.

It was just a single-minded desire to walk and leave the world behind me, and that was all I focused on.

I was not without money but in my single-minded

mission to escape my society I had been only driven by the thought of freedom, neglecting much-needed sleep and a proper meal.

I was weak and tired, my delicate appearance looked even more fragile and where there once was a beautifully defined body was now a thin skeleton of my former self. I looked as drained and grey as the landscape, and yet as I looked at my hands, they seemed to shine their pale glow, for I was still so white in comparison to the grey city. How the city differed from where I came from struck me hard as I walked towards its suburbs, none of the green parks and fantastic architecture, instead what looked like metal boxes stacked high with chimneys spewing black smoke. It looked like pictures I had seen of factories and slum towns back before the wars.

How could people live like this?

These houses were smaller than the rooms I had walked through in the opera house. The streets were dark, empty, and the chill from the winter breezes was only amplified down wind tunnels created by the tightly packed buildings. No one was out, it was too cold, and even I in a well-made coat with its fur lining could feel the cold, so those less fortunate to afford such a luxury would definitely not stand to be out in the streets now. I felt guilty all of a sudden. I realised how out of place I would look here; it wouldn't take much to realise I was an aristocrat.

I turned, feeling foolish.

How could I have thought that this place would offer me salvation? My complexion itself seemed to glow in the face of dark and dirty streets. I walked a while heading towards the river I could hear flowing nearby, but now I was genuinely alone; my attempt to escape drowning in the icy water I was approaching. I had nowhere to go, I was lost. Then I saw her, a young girl broke the surface of the river. Fear and panic blazed in her eyes as she realised much like I did in the same instant that she must have fallen into that icy grave. It did not take long for me to decide what to do as I ran to the river calling out to her in some hope she would hear me as if that alone meant she was going to be ok, that my attempt to save her would succeed and with no response from her I dived in.

The water was as cold as the empty spot in my heart, and I knew that in my weakened state I may not escape this, but at least I could try and save her. The current ripped around us as I tried to pull up keeping her head above the surface and for what seemed like an eternity, we battled with the water, it trying to pull us down, me trying to pull us up. Water filled my lungs making it hard to breathe. It tasted of soot from the chimneys and mud from the banks as it stung my eyes, making it impossible to see. Then I noticed the debris, who knows what had been dumped into this river but I knew one of us was about to collide with it, I had to use what strength I had left in me.

I turned us in the river my back colliding with a crash into the floating mass, it was solid, and I winced as I felt something sharp pierce my side.

If it had not been for the fact that my body had become numb from being in this river, I knew the pain would have been worse. I was silently thankful that I would not know how hurt I had been otherwise I wouldn't have been able to drag us out.

With one arm around the girl, I used the other to grab hold of the debris slowly dragging myself along it until I was near enough the bank to grasp that. At first, I came away with handfuls of mud but soon I was able to hold on enough to drag us both from our disappointed icy grave. I tried to use my legs but it was useless, they were tired from kicking and had become numb, so I used my arm to pull us up the bank, mud collecting on our clothes and hair until we were out enough to relax. I panted heavily, my body heavy with exhaustion hoping someone would find us, that this child would be okay as I draped an arm around her so that at least some of my body heat could warm her.

My eyes grew heavy, and I was aware of the feeling of something warm slowly soaking into my torn clothes where I had hit the debris. I retreated into the knowledge that I would not wake up, but maybe it was for the best; I had nothing left to live for, nowhere to go and at least in my dreams I could see the one person who could have cared.

And with that as my last thought, I drifted into unconsciousness into my peaceful dream world.

———

I came to, woken by the soft sound of sobbing.

It was strange, I had not expected to survive, but here I was in a bed warm and safe. I could hear the girl talking into the embrace of a man who must be her father I was glad she had made it, I wanted so much to have succeeded, and I did. With that, I tried to sit up, but now that my body was no longer numb I could feel the pain rip into my side as I tried to hide my apparent frailty. I could tell she saw the wince; it was hard to hide it in my eyes, and as I sat up I let my covers slip. I had not realised my clothes had been removed, but it made sense since I now had bandages on and was in a warm bed. But the minute they fell I wished I had stayed lying down.

The look of shock in her face, no one could have hidden. It was the look I feared that look of how of silent realisation that I was not how I appeared. I couldn't bear the gaze. I felt like whatever part of me had saved her was being ripped away because of my deceiving appearance and I tried to gather my covers to hide my traitorous body. I was ashamed that her saviour couldn't be what she wanted as I softly spoke to express the gratitude she was alive.

I lay back down.

I couldn't stand being stared at, and the pain in my side was growing stronger. I wanted to cry, weep like some little child but that only made me feel even more insecure. There was a soft sound, footsteps leaving the room but I still felt her presence there beside me. Then she spoke, a small voice at first gaining more confidence as she thanked me, asked me to turn and face her. It was kind and innocent, she really was thankful I had saved her, and she was sorry that she had made me feel bad. I knew my own insecurities brought me down, that it was easy for my appearance to be misinterpreted.

I shouldn't really be upset with a girl who had just escaped death herself, so I turned to her as she spoke calling me an angel. It touched my heart, those words. Many had referred to my mother like that and as such the comparison had also been lavished on me but never with this innocent sincerity and even though my body hurt, I turned. Never had someone spoken to me like that, it was the first time I felt sincerity, that someone was glad to see me. It was the first time since he had looked at me that it felt like someone was looking at the real me.

I thanked her. I could see the small blush on her cheeks, a sweet smile to my words which turned to a look of curiosity. So we talked, explaining who I was, how I had come to be here. It was refreshing to talk to someone who didn't want something from you. I felt relaxed and peaceful for once, happy. We were both thinking the same thing, it was evident in her eyes. I'm sure the same look was in mine to finally have someone to talk to who understood. She didn't judge anything I said, even when I spoke of times I had dated other men she found it amusing.

We shared something in common.

After a while our conversation began to ebb, she brightened up, a look of joy in her face as she asked me to stay and I accepted. In the end, I found someone to talk to, somewhere to stay. I suddenly felt like I was about to learn what it meant to have a family.

And with that, she left to tell her parents and so I could rest as I was beginning to feel tired from the emotional conversation. My life seemed to have changed. I was accepted somewhere. I was going to be able to grow and live a real life, not just relying on my dreams. I had escaped, but part of me was still missing. Something or someone, maybe in this city.

I would see those eyes again, but now it was less desperate, now I had other things to live for than a chance meeting with a distant memory.

Chapter 6

Cain

THE SUN WITHOUT A SKY

Being at the opera house didn't seem worth it now he no longer dwelled there.

I thought it was best that he left to discover the world and who he was for himself and who knows how long I could have resisted the temptation I saw in him? My room was a mess, the mansion I lived in cold, dark, not a fireplace or candle had been lit in it since he left. I was so sure he would have come back by now, maybe it was better this way. Every room, corridor and staircase was bathed in darkness and cold, the place felt like a prison rather than a home, it was a tomb, I may as well be dwelling in a casket in a graveyard somewhere rather than living like this. Although I had not seen my reflection for many years, every mirror lay broken. Who cared about superstition? Seven years of bad luck compared to hundreds of years alone or even a year without him. Fragments of glass lay everywhere; I kept thinking I had kept them so when he returned to me, he could admire his beauty once more before his reflection was gone and only through my eyes he would see how beautiful he was.

What a silly romantic idea. I should have known better to have let my desire grow this much.

I couldn't face myself; curtains lay torn from their windows, so it made it difficult to move about my own home during the day.

Furniture was smashed; my own anger grew strong, even my feeding grew more violent, not the same soft seduction I once played. I now was violent, taking too much blood, which only made me stronger and more restless. No more delicate feedings; I stalked victims through the night. I couldn't bear to step into that building, so empty now, so I had to find my prey like the rest of my kind. Dragging defenceless women down alleys, the look of pure fear on their faces as they struggled. It was useless, once I had them in my grasp there was no escape as I bit into them, let the blood flow freely. It spilt, soaking my clothes and pooling at my feet, then I would let them go, watch them crawl into the street screaming for help as I disappeared into the night.

Soon the papers were filled with stories of women being brutally attacked; so far no deaths but who knows how long it would take the killer to escalate. I realised that if my behaviour continued I would be found out, someone would realise, come to kill me, rid the world of such an ancient menace. I didn't care, so what if they found me? I had lived enough and when I finally found something I wanted it, was gone. I had lived for him, lived with the hope I would someday own him that he would come to me, but he had chosen to escape the world we lived in. Maybe I would let it end, if obsession and loneliness didn't drive me mad first, it would be better to let go of this life.

Even a cursed man deserves his end. I was tired of living this nightmare. I finally learned to love someone else, and I had been denied, I was too caught up in my own desire and needs to ever approach him, to confront him with my feelings to see if this love could be returned, and so I had done nothing.

A light flickered outside in the streets, another search party prowling the city looking for the monster in the dark. They may be aristocrats, but they weren't used to this; they lived sheltered lives, had servants for their every need and whim. What did they know of hunting a prey they didn't even understand? Maybe it would be amusing to join the hunt, watch them worry and panic at little noises in the dark, it would at least humour me for a while. Or maybe I could ambush them; a massacre would bring in someone professional, someone a bit more fun to play with until I was finally put out of my misery. It only fitted that someone formed from bloodlust, lived through blood would die from the blood.

I could gorge on their bodies till my body could drink no more, but gluttony seemed like such a cheap way to set about my release. Indeed, the only person I would have wanted to die for, the only person I would have allowed to end me would be him. I wanted the one I lived for to be the one I died for, the last thing I saw before I bled into ashes.

He had given me my first real taste of what it meant to live, so to speak, and I wanted him to be the one to release my body like he did my heart, but even that hope was far away now.

I was hungry; I needed to feed. If I couldn't fulfil one desire, I would at least feed the other basic desire.

I left the house again into the dark streets watching the still world, waiting for movement until I heard a scream. I could smell blood in the air, only faintly, but also the odour of the dead, not the quality of a high-class vampire but of young and foolish creatures. I turned the corner; there they stood, three of them pushing the frightened girl between them, taunting her, trying to decide who would bite first. It was sad; it reminded me of a rabbit caught by a hunting pack. I hated them, no class and I realised that was what I would turn into if I continued; it was sickening. I shouted out to them demanding to know what they were doing in my hunting ground.

"We heard about the attacks, figured the rules here had changed and that it was an open buffet. Can't blame us, sounds like you haven't been acting your pretentious self; seemed safe enough for us to come here, maybe join you in this little dining frenzy you're beginning to create. What do you say, friend?"

I felt insulted they thought I was like them now, that they could just come here, join me. 'Disgusting', I whispered to myself but knew they heard. I saw their eyes light up with anger, baring their teeth. If they wanted to fight so be it, let's see how these children of the night faced an actual creature of the night.

"Dear boys, if you want to dine here you should learn some manners, how about respect your elders or respect someone who could kill you where you stand before you had a chance to run in fear."

They didn't like my words. Youngsters are so easy, a simple invitation and they have to prove their strength. They pounced, the girl dropping to the floor to escape the ensuing fight; she remained there frozen in terror. I needed a good fight, though it would get some rage out of my system if they had only known how unfortunate they were. Before they had reached me I had used my own force to push them to the ground.

I sneered, taunting them, that they should realise what it meant to attack an elder and that I didn't want to get my hands dirty from them. Oh, how they howled; it was fun watching, their features smooth into the pavement beneath them before I released them. They crawled for a bit, desperate for breath. I picked one up, broke his neck before he could even look at me, the ash flowing about carried by the night air, how easy. He had been the one that had called me 'friend', a little rough looking, not the seductive attractiveness a vampire should have. His hair was messy and lank, and he wore the clothes of a much younger city, a period with no style or taste as far as I was concerned. He gave my kind a bad name, looking so ugly and ill-dressed.

The second stood; I laughed as he ran at me. Then he came to a sudden stop, blood splattered on my cheek. I used one hand to wipe it off, the other I removed from his chest as he slumped to the floor and dissipated to ash. If he had been better looking than his friend I wouldn't have known; his face was half crushed from my first assault, the remains of his features squashed into the pavement he had been crushed in to. He looked like a living corpse, bloody and ugly, chunks of his face missing and a gaping wound for a cheek, revealing broken teeth. I didn't even register what he was wearing, to try and place his age or origin; I couldn't have cared less about this carcass that had thrown itself at me.

So predictable, the third started to run away shouting something about me being a monster. How amusing, this was doing me good. From the back he had a good figure, clearly kept himself a little better than his fallen colleague, tight jeans, a fitted t-shirt and his hair was cut close, short and well managed. Shame, he could have been handsome, but his face was only going to reflect fear and horror, twisting through any finer features he may have had. Before he even made it three steps, I was in front of him, drawing the now blooded hand to my mouth and licking it.

"Disgusting," I sneered again.

He turned to run, but yet again I stood before him. I bet he felt just like the woman frozen on the floor; she had passed out after I had killed the first one. He begged, pleaded, it was pathetic, trying to explain that vampires weren't meant to kill their own, but as I stated, there was nothing similar between us, I was superior to him in every way, we were not of the same kind. He turned. How stupid; my hands clawed across his back piercing his flesh creating deep cuts. He fell, blood spilling at my feet.

He tried to crawl away, that would not do, and since my shoes were already ruined, I didn't overthink about crushing his skull beneath them until ash clung to the blood on them. It had felt good to let go, take out my frustration, to indulge such a basic desire. It didn't matter who they were, it was kind of like I had just done the human world a service, all I had to do was worry about the girl.

I had no idea where she lived, so I did the only thing I could think of, I took her home and laid her in a bed so she could sleep. She was an attractive girl, slim and elegant, brown hair had fallen from its clasps from being pushed about. Her skin smooth, light brown but so different from Yue-ren's pale complexion. I left her; it was no good for me to stare at something I had willingly taken home, she would be gone tomorrow, so I retired to my room. It was then I dreamed, a dream I had many times, a dream of him, a dream that was the only part of him I had left now, but a dream that always ended the same.

———

I t was dark and cold, so much of my life was.

I could hear singing, a beautiful melody, it could only be his voice, nothing else could draw me so. Soft light shone like candlelight illuminating his face and slowly his body. How I envied the light for being so close to him, to be able to caress his body like that. He stood on water, which rippled around his feet; his reflection looked like it was dancing on the surface of whatever pool he was standing on. His eyes looked at me, beckoning me to him, to join him, to hold him. I knew he wanted me as much as I wanted him. But as I stepped on to the water, he fell through, plunging himself into the depths sending droplets through the air and sending everything into silence. I ran to the spot he fell, but the pool began to ice over until a smooth surface separated us.

I beat the surface with my hands, cried out to him, scratching at the surface. I could see him drown, his clothes clung to him, and his hair swam around his face as he moved in slow motion. It was beautiful but so painful; his arms outstretched to me, hoping I would grab them, pull him into my safe embrace but I could not. My body was getting cold and numb from crouching on the ice my hand red and raw from beating the surface. I felt tears in my eyes but the minute they left my eyes they were swept away by the wind, snowflakes in the night as I screamed for him.

I woke with a start panting heavily, and I could feel the sweat on my brow and back as strands of hair clung to me. Through the blond mass that cascaded around me, I saw her at the end of my bed staring back at me.

"I heard you scream out; I came to see if you were okay and to thank you for saving me."

As she spoke, she walked closer, brown eyes that matched her brown hair that was now loose and free-flowing swaying about her as she walked until she stopped before me.

"You called for Yue-ren, the opera mistress' daughter. To cry out her name in your sleep means you must have loved her greatly. Yue-ren is very lucky that someone so willing to save a stranger's life holds her in such regard." She continued.

"Whatever you heard, disregard it. My affection for Yue-ren is none of your concern or mine for that matter since she no longer resides within the Opera house." I replied not quite able to remove the tinge of regret and loneliness in my voice.

Upon hearing this, she must have picked up the tone in my voice, and there was pity in her eyes. I hated her a little then, how could a human girl pity a creature such as myself.

"Sir, I am sorry she has left, and it's clear you are lonely without her. I don't have anything to offer in the way of thanks, but I would happily listen to you talk if you so desire it," she added.

I laughed inwardly. Really, this naïve creature wanted to comfort me, offer solace and think me some poor jilted lover.

"I assure you, I have no need for your words. Be gone with you girl, talk does not warm one's bed, it does not place tender kisses to one's lips, and I fear you cannot offer such comforts." I explained.

"Then as a thank you, I will offer you a kiss for rescuing me, you seem a man of far more character and worth than those who attacked me."

She was naïve, or maybe not, maybe she knew more about men's hearts and desire, how to play with their wants and needs. It was something I had seen countless times; women who found men that would be able to give them the lives they wanted, whether that be fame, fortune or safety.

"And what of my cold bed? If you do not want to find yourself devoured, then I suggest you leave. I am not so good of character that I will stop with a kiss." With this, I thought I had put the matter to rest. I did not need her pity or her kisses. If she were a naïve girl, this would tell her the danger she was still in, and if she was a shrewd temptress, I would resist and throw her out. Maybe because I was genuinely lonely and not myself for it seemed as if I was the naïve one as she sat on my bed.

I wanted to resist, but she had already kissed me, and my desire and frustration were too intense to ignore as I pulled her into my bed. Her body was not innocent, it was wanting as I devoured her flesh. She didn't have the delicate frame of Yue-ren, she had very much the round hips and full breasts of a woman and her skin was warmer, her eyes gleamed with want, none of the innocence he had, none of his delicacy as she clung to me, drawing her nails across her back. Yes, she was every bit the clever temptress. She was revelling in it there was no sweet seduction, it wasn't gentle or loving, it was simple want.

This was not making love, this was sex, and it was wrong, it was dirty and cheap, and she was not him, she couldn't compare. I hated her; I wished I had let those vampires feed off her, kill her. She was dirtying me, making me cheap in the place of the person I really wanted here. My eyes glowed in the dark, vicious and cruel as I bit down into her; if she wanted it brutal, I was going to allow her that one pleasure. I pinned her arms to the bed the blood from her neck staining my pillow as she looked into my face the lust turned to fear as she noticed my eyes and the sudden realisation of what I was shifted to panic, but she had chosen her fate.

I bit; I fed until she had no strength to struggle until I could feed no more, until the body that had writhed beneath me lay still, never to move again. I had killed her.

She was the first I had killed in many years.

I screamed, crawling from the bed, ripping covers as I went. If there was anything left to destroy I tore it apart, my rage uncontrolled; I was nothing more than a rabid beast. The only thing that had any hold on me was him, I had to find him. I had to atone; I needed him to accept me, to save me. I had gone beyond lust, desire and obsession, it was something more. He was my salvation, either to love me or kill me; it would release me from my torture. I decided to leave, I would find him no matter what, I would tell him everything, I would offer him the salvation from his loneliness, I would prove that I loved the real him and that we could save each other, it was time to stop living in shadows.

It was time to go to him.

Chapter 7

Yue-ren

A BRIGHT MOON ON THE RISE

IT HAD BEEN A WHILE SINCE COMING HERE TO ANNABEL and her parents' home, but I had never regretted it.

At first, I was too ill to even get out of bed. I had let myself deteriorate and wither, so my immune system was low. It was no surprise that being exposed to such cold weather and water meant I had caught pneumonia. Annabel's parents had nursed me; her mother was kind, everything a mother should have been, hardworking and supportive; even her name seems to fit her personality, Joy. She had worked hard nursing me with home cooked meals and a warm place to stay. Matthew, Annabel's father, was a strong man and a patient one. He never complained about carrying me about the house like a child, and soon the embarrassment of my burden faded as a realised that they felt indebted to me for saving Annabel. I gave them the jewellery I wore; it was sold with enough profit for my medication, food and many comforts they lacked before, like extra firewood and blankets.

It surprised me how they never spent unnecessarily; only on what they needed. It meant the money from my jewellery would go far. After a while, I began to feel at home.

As for Annabel, she stayed by my bedside talking to me about anything she could think of. She must have been alone for such a long time to have so much conversation in her, or maybe for once, she felt relaxed enough around someone to share her thoughts and feelings. I spoke too, letting my own tales pour out to her ever-listening presence. She loved the stories of my life in aristocratic society, balls, parties, dinners, opera and the men and women who resided there. I had told her my story and she never once judged me or looked down upon me, we were equals. Once I began to recover, my wound healed and the tiredness fading, I began to sing for her. How she loved it, the look of happiness she wore upon her face, even her mother would come and listen.

They always had the highest praise for my voice. Soon my figure had returned to me; I was back to that elegant form, and although Matthew joked that I needed more meat on my bones, an honest joke from a man brought up in a hardworking lifestyle, he never tried to enforce it on me. It was as if he understood how important my looks and physique were to me.

Soon I was able to move about the house; Joy had made me clothes from material she bought with the leftover money; a soft cloth, smooth against my skin. The material made a shirt that sat slightly off my shoulders and hung longer than a shirt should, with bell sleeves, all in all very elegant. It was the kind of shirt that I would wear, not a woman's shirt but more feminine than a man's shirt, it was a shirt just for me, and I loved the fact that she knew me enough to make such a thing. Joy herself worked as a seamstress in a local shop; she was quite the talent and while her clothes were simple compared to the fashion boutiques that had made up New London's shopping districts they were made with more love and emotion than any dress I had ever worn. No, her shop was a labour of love, to make good clothes, clothes that would survive the conditions and work these people were used to. Clothes that were made for comfort and longevity and yet had a personal feel, a warm and friendly vision as if they were as much made of hope, love and compassion as they were of cotton and threads.

Annabel would brush my hair she said it was what she imagined silk would feel like, so when I suggested cutting it so I wouldn't stand out so much in public, she threw such a fuss I decided just to keep it in a ponytail when I eventually was able to leave the house to go about the town.

I now had no problem with my appearance, and my insecurities seemed so unjustified around them, they judged me as a person, and as Matthew always commented, it didn't matter my background or my past, it didn't matter how I chose to look or conduct myself, it all made up who I am. Most importantly he said that my worth as a person was already measured that day I saved his daughter's life and if that didn't make me a man of worth, nothing would. As far as he was concerned, I was welcome to stay with them as long as I wanted and to be part of his family.

The city they lived in began to change around me; it wasn't so cold and intimidating. Yes, the colours were limited to metallic greys and rusted browns. Many of the taller structures tinged black at the top from the smoke from the factory areas. The ground was always muddy, and dark water would snake down paths. The sun would reflect off the metal walls sometimes causing a golden shine from the rust that tinted them. But this city was the opposite of where I had lived, which may have been beautiful to behold but the people were vapid and warped.

This city was filled with good people, and it was their individual characteristics that made this city, not the walls that they had built around them. It took a while to get used to the lack of architecture and an increase in all the things the aristocrats complained about. The city was noisy and dirty; the smell of metal and rust, the ever-present smog that tinged tall structures black and left the air smelling burnt, but it was real, not just a pretty picture. In fact, I began to prefer this world for the simple reason that here the people were honest to themselves, never pretending to be someone else. They worked hard and survived on their own strengths and talents. It was not always a safe place, I knew that crime was evident; I'm not so naïve to think that everyone here is a good person but I also knew that these were crimes committed by people desperate to make their lives better or simply stealing food to survive.

Somehow these crimes seemed more justified than the sins of passion, wants and decadence. Some still taunted me for my appearance, but at least they recognised me as a feminine male rather than a woman. Their insults hurt much less than anything else I had gone through. I had learnt to be cold and distant, and some of that still remained in me, enough to disregard the comments of such people.

Living in a home with such love, patience and understanding it was no wonder my heart had begun to thaw.

It was this thawing that also made me more aware of another emotion I had hidden deep inside me, a feeling that came whenever I thought of those eyes looking at me in the dark. Even here I could not escape that look of passion and desire, an examination of someone who genuinely wanted me. I was learning to love; Annabel was like a sister, we grew close very fast, but it was in the way a friendship would. I looked out for her, listened to her, and she did the same for me. We would go shopping together, and I'd advise her on clothes and jewellery. It was fun; she was only a few years younger than I was, so our tastes weren't dissimilar. We would even notice an attractive man; give them scores out of ten, I felt like a teenager. I had never acted like this before; so much had been about being proper. Annabel once said I was like a big sister, even though she still told her friends at school that I was a guardian angel sent to look after her and her family.

But alas even with all this warmth and kindness, still I still wished for something more, something I was missing. I wanted to be loved. Truly loved, now that I was more confident, now I was free to be myself, I wanted nothing more for him to find me, now I was ready. I thought at first my new life would have extinguished these feelings, that being part of a real family would chase away these desires. But now I lacked past insecurities I knew who I was and it didn't scare me anymore. I decided to get a job, help earn my keep with Joy and Matthew but also be able to make some money to get Annabel through school. She had told me so many times what a proper education would mean, how it was a ticket to freedom to making her own life.

But I had another reason, and though it seemed silly and unlikely, I wanted to work somewhere public where many people gathered in the hope that one day I would encounter him.

It wasn't hard; my appearance was a draw to many women and men alike, and my voice was much praised, so the local tavern gave me a job there. I was to serve drinks and food and when needed, sing for the guests. It turned out that stories of the local angel had spread and my singing seemed to bring much comfort and joy to the people of this city. A woman once said my voice sounded like hope; hearing me sing gave her confidence to continue to try her hardest to live well. Someone also said that it was worth working through the day so that they could come to hear me sing in the evening. It was amazing, I no longer sang for flattery and vanity, for an audience that took my presence for granted, I sang to people who truly appreciated the gift of such a song.

Soon I spent most of my time singing in the tavern making many friends both male and female and earning the money that sent Annabel to school and kept our home. It was with great pride that I could call it our home, well cared for and provided for.

It was strange; women would ask me how I kept my figure so well and my hair so soft and long. Sometimes they asked for advice with clothes and jewellery while younger women would just naturally blush as I spoke to them. Men asked me how I was able to keep the attention of women so well but were never bitter about it. People knew me now as I am and just like Annabel's parents they no longer judged me, even when it was made public that I was not so tempted by the women that befriended me. The women were disappointed, and the men found it amusing that all their efforts to court me had been in vain. It was a relief that it did not threaten them, these people were so much more openminded; even some of the young men came out of their shells to ask me out.

But I saw it in their eyes that they had just been drawn to my looks rather than me being a male. It was easy to make them understand their own feelings; they were smitten, not in love. And yet I still waited for him, the one whose eyes held the truth, whose eyes held a passion like none other.

———

Time kept moving, and many events happened. Soon enough, it was Annabel's eighteenth birthday; such a grand affair, nothing like the balls of the opera house.

People sang and drank together, there weren't rules to behave. The tavern was filled that night, the regulars had taught me new songs, local tunes to sing and I had taught them dances so that the young men were all well prepared to sweep Annabel off her feet as they danced. It was so carefree and fun, just cheerful rather than conceited conversation and bragging about the expense of their latest item of clothing or jewellery purchased for that night. The men had taught me to dance with them, dances of such energy that no matter how hard I tried I would stumble or fall. These dances had none of the graceful elegance I was used to, and usually involved linking arms and prancing about the place, making as much noise as possible. I still liked my more graceful dances, my time here had not changed that, I still drank red wine in a ladylike manner and moved with grace; people knew my femininity would never change, but at least I could join in, and they would include me in their celebrations.

On my twenty-second birthday we had had a proper sit-down dinner, everyone wore his or her best clothes, really dressing up for the occasion. It was so touching the effort they went to; to make my day special, the kind of affair I was used to. The tavern had been filled with white flowers made of material; they could not afford real flowers nor was this the place that would grow them well, but they all donated a piece of white cloth to Joy who made them into flowers, this gesture more moving. These flowers would last forever, never to wither and die, never be thrown out for rotting, just simply be able to bloom perfectly forever. Everyone was trying so hard to be gracious, it made me laugh. They were working so hard to embrace that side of me, making sure my birthday was as elegant and graceful as I was.

In the end, I told them I liked them best when they were themselves and my birthday became another loud and energetic affair. Everyone had learnt my dances, but in the hands of my new friends and family, they soon turned from graceful displays of movement to what looked like a mess of out of control spinning tops. A stylish turn that was supposed to sweep the woman round with you, when too energetic, sent many a couple spinning and tumbling. I will never forget how I laughed that night, how happy I was. I wish I had realised that someone like me was not meant to be that happy.

If had known what was to come maybe I could have let my heart ice over again because it surprises me how quickly a thawed heart could break.

Chapter 8

Cain

THE ENCROACHING STORM AND
WANDERING SUN

HE SEEMED SO HAPPY NOW, MY DEAR LITTLE BOY, looking so radiant in his new life.

But he had been very naughty leaving the opera house and putting years of work to waste. Ever since he was born, I had plans for him. He was going to be my greatest creation, fulfil my greatest desire. I had worked hard to keep his heart frozen and his soul as pale as his beautiful skin. He was always in solitude, and his eyes were like blue tinted glass, no sparkle of life. Now they blazed with joy, compassion and happiness, no desperation, no despair. What was I going to do with a puppet whose soul was beginning to develop? Such a nurturing environment was un-weaving the tapestry I had made for him. He had, at least, kept innocent so I had something I could still manipulate, but his fears were gone. These people were so accepting of him. His background didn't threaten them, and he never felt that he was above them, they were equals.

My sweet, sweet boy; beautiful, innocent, graceful and so pure I wanted him, I wanted to take all that and create the object of want I craved so much. But these people were saving him from himself with their acceptance and love. They needed his gifts, enjoyed his company, and most of all opened the heart I had wanted to keep sealed. Well, the game had gone on long enough; it was time to change the rules. He had had his fun, and a bit of freedom but Yue-ren was born for me and was mine alone, I would not share him. He was supposed to sink into darkness, allow me to devour him, smother him in my world of torture and emptiness. But his little escape had put a dent in my plans, though I could have made my move sooner if I hadn't thought of the perfect punishment for him trying to leave me.

I let him live here; lulled into a false sense of security that his life was improving and he had found a home, but he didn't realise his home was with me. This tavern he sang in was warm and friendly, no place for someone who is supposed to be distant and despairing. I had come here a lot to watch him, choosing many guises for myself. I had danced with his precious Annabel; he was trying so hard to make sure she had a good life. I had danced with him as a simple girl clinging close to him, taking the secret delight in being so close to his body while pretending to be just another blushing fan. I would let him have this last night, this birthday brawl that made him oh so happy but tomorrow it would be time to come back to me. It was time for his life to go back down the path I had chosen for him. The joy in this place was beginning to make me sick, I needed somewhere dark and quiet, I couldn't look at how they had corrupted my prey. I needed solitude for a while. I left into the night to find a spot to go over all the delightfully morbid thoughts of death, misery and pain that were to come, tomorrow was going to be fun.

I found another bar; it was cold and dark with only a few people in it drinking alone in silence, a perfect place for me to sit and think. The silence was pleasant, and the barmen kept to himself; an old man with a tired expression who simply poured my drink and left me alone without a word. I chose the darkest corner and sat feeling the very darkness ease my being, the smell of lost hope-filled this place. The souls of the lonely are so easily read, and I could simply sit here, the pathetic energy of those who had given up on themselves was better than any drink I could let touch my lips. And then he walked in, I smelt the blood on him, and I knew the minute he entered; Vampire.

Not just any vampire, he was an old vampire who had probably lived through many centuries of mankind. I could almost feel the power that flowed through him. He was firm but more than that, beautiful, more so than many a man, long wavy blonde hair, even when tied back, cascaded about him like waves and an intense stare. What raw sexual power and what an imposing figure of a man. His voice was rich and sensual, if he had been human I would have loved to have let him seduce me, but his soul was already tortured and full of sin, maybe his heart was as dark as mine. He chose a spot by the fireplace with its dying embers casting a red light across his features and clothes, clothes of aristo-cratic society, he was definitely an ancient beast to afford such luxury but why would he be here in such a low-class city? As he sipped his drink, I saw the look in his eyes, full of thought, the expression knitting across his brow.

As I watched, I wished I were in a different guise rather than that of an average city dweller, then maybe I would have looked at least like someone who he would accept company from. I wanted to know what could bring such a creature here. I felt the energy from him, his bloodlust was strong. Some great desire must have brought him here, something was torturing this man, and then I recognised it, the same fervour that drove me. It was not something that had brought him here, but someone, this vampire was in love. I could see the passion in those eyes, a passion that bordered on madness. Lust for more than blood, a need to own whomever it was he had come in search for. I decided no matter what I looked like, I had to talk to him; it's not every day that one meets someone with the same lust and driving desire.

I approached slowly; I should have known an ancient would have recognised me for what I was, as quickly as I had recognised him.

"I have nothing to say to you demon, go find someone else to torment tonight."

"My, we are in a bad mood, but I'm not here to torment you. It appears we have a common desire; I read your energy and it's as easy to recognise as the smell of blood on you."

He looked at me, not letting a single emotion on his face get through as if my words meant nothing. He was calm and focused, allowing nothing betray the desire I saw deep in his eternal soul. His hand reached out gracefully until he had my face in his grasp, fingers resting on my cheek, pulling me closer. His eyes were intensely burning into me, his grip growing tighter; if I had been human, he would have left bruises. His nails scraped into my skin, I felt blood warm against my cheek.

At first, I thought he was going to crush my skull there and then, so I was about to argue my case. Any good demon knew how to sweet talk themselves out of any situation, but those powers were less strong against other creatures of the night. Then he let go, licking my blood from his fingertips. How many people he must have seduced, he was good, but I knew what he had been studying my face for.

He saw the truth, he read the same desire and lust, the same secret passion, he had apparently not wanted to trust the words of a demon, but I was as good at my games as he was his. I let my eyes betray that little bit of emotion that we both shared. I rested into the seat opposite as he offered a glass of the wine he had been sipping, inviting conversation. I had got his interest.

"This love must be strong that you dirty yourself by coming to such a place. I know what desire feels like; I know what it is like to crave a mortal. It's a craving that no human can understand, a passion only beings such as us can have. Only those who know true sin can appreciate something as pure as an innocent soul."

Still no change in his features, but he was listening; I had hit the spot, I wish I knew what he thought as I spoke. We soon began a conversation, a little small talk, about humans, how they amused us mainly, but also a bit of the love of a pure human soul and once in a lifetime love for creatures such as ourselves. We spoke of how this city was so dark and uninteresting; it had no flavour like those of the aristocracy. We talked about how this new world made our existence so much easier, small safe topics, nothing personal or of considerable note. We spoke of many similar things till he excused himself, I was not about to impose on him anymore.

A good demon knows when to back away when to let a dangerous creature of such power as an ancient vampire dictate the terms of social interaction. If you anger a beast, you are sure to get yourself torn to pieces, and this particular beast had all the power in the world to make even a demon cower in fright and experience true pain and death. As much as I wanted to know of this love he spoke of, I knew it was different to mine, but I knew better than to cross such a powerful creature of the night. A good demon knows what battles to fight and when to speak. There was something a bit different to this vampire's love. As much as

I could see the love and the will to be with the one he desired, he was holding himself back as if he wanted to protect this love. Oh how I wanted to solve this puzzle, but alas, now was not the time. After all, tomorrow was an important day; I had much to plan, I couldn't be distracted by a vampire that had given his heart to a mortal, it was taboo such a pairing, but it would have been entertaining to watch the pain they would have to go through.

Oh, what beautiful suffering I could witness if my intuition were right. But I had my own obsession, I had to prepare for when Yue-ren returned to me, tomorrow was going to be such a beautiful day.

———

The demon had been easy to spot, and I would have liked it if he had stayed far away from me, I was in no mood for company.

But alas, he came over, and I tried to dismiss him. Even in a place like this, I would not demean myself by associating with something as foul as a demon. Even its smell offended me, and the people here were lucky not to notice the odour of lies, deceit and sadistic pleasure; no fragrance in the human world can mask the smell of evil intention. Then the unexpected happened; he talked of desire, and I was instantly curious to know how easy it was for this monster to read me. As I clasped his face, I read the look in his eyes, demons were not to be trusted and I had to be sure this wasn't some game. I saw it in his eyes, passion, lust and the desire to own a mortal, so I let him speak.

He slunk into a chair in front of me, and I offered him a glass of wine, I must be getting weak to allow such company, but it's not always that you meet someone who holds that same secret inside. For us dwellers of the dark we live for the hunt, for lust and cravings, for taking what we want, we don't share our feelings or desires, so it is unheard of that two such beasts as a vampire, and a demon share a common thought or wish.

And so conversation began, at first not saying a word, merely letting his smooth tongue divulge what it was he wanted to speak of. A polite discussion of shared interests and opinion of this city and world we live in, I was waiting for him to pry more out of me, after all, he was a demon, where would the fun be for him if he didn't try and get something from this conversation. He was curious and inquisitive, and I eventually began to respond back, nothing detailed just simply understandings of what it meant to have a human consume our thoughts. I didn't let much slip, never spoke Yue-ren's name, as it was sacred to me. Neither of us named the people who had captured our immortal souls, no real details such as their sex or what they looked like.

After all, we didn't need to discuss what they looked like, it wasn't why they had drawn us to them, it was the emotions inside we shared, not the person. So we talked of how cruel fate was, to be separated from what you believe is yours, the anger, the rage of not being with the one you crave.

The conversation was civil, but we soon started to discuss how other temptations and desires seemed to pale in comparison. It was then I realised the difference between us; as much as I desired Yue-ren, however strong the desire to poses him, I would never force him, I was willing to let him kill me rather than live without him. I loved him; I believed we were destined to be together but that he would give himself to me willingly not through deceit or seduction and certainly without pain. But this demon wanted to break whoever haunted him so, wanted to own and devour, watch all beauty and grace leave this mortal. He wasn't in love with the person; he was in love with the desire of what he could do to them.

I felt sorry for this person of desire, how bleak the outcome looked for them, no human could escape a demon's grasp; once their soul belonged to a demon, it would never know happiness again. But there was only one human I cared for, and I was not about to get in the way of a demon's plan. After all, demons made dangerous enemies, I wasn't about to lose sight of my goals for a human I had never met and experience the misfortune of crossing a demon's path.

Once I finished my glass I bid my farewell, the night was calling me, and I had tired of such distrustful company. He looked a little hurt that I had not answered all his questions, but he recognised the same fear of crossing an ancient vampire's path, so didn't stand in the way of my parting.

Off into the night, I walked, hoping our paths would never cross again and thinking only of Yue-ren and what tomorrow would bring for I knew deep inside that that was the day we would see each other again. I felt it in my blood.

Chapter 9

THE MOON THAT SHONE TOO BRIGHT

IT WAS A WARM DAY WHEN I AWOKE, A GENTLE BREEZE waved through my open window, and light beams rested across my bed.

It is lucky I do not drink as much as the people in this city as my head would have hurt too much to enjoy this morning. Poor Annabel, she must be feeling terrible; she had done my share of celebrating last night, I had to carry her home. I knew that Matthew was out early today, he had gone to the factory to help with installing a new furnace; it was, after all, that time of year when all the old was repaired and replaced. Joy would also be going out; she wanted to test the new machines at the sewing mill. It had been all she talked of for two weeks; a device that could sew faster than a person, somehow this little town was prospering, and invention was coming into their lives. Annabel would not be up for hours, but she had said she'd join me for lunch today when she woke up. I went to work. It was such an ordinary day until I met him while walking through the streets.

He was tall, black hair tied in a ponytail and green eyes,

quite handsome. He looked like a factory worker but carried himself proud and confident. At first, I thought he was waiting for me, but that was impossible since we had never met before now.

"Nice day, my pretty boy."

He smiled at me, kind and gentle, stretching out his hand and shaking mine, although I swear his smile turned into a small sneer, but it was quick to appear and disappear from his features. He did not let go, I felt his thumb graze gently over mine, and then he withdrew his hand from mine. I felt a little confused as to why he was suddenly making himself known to me and in the manner that the men back at the opera house would as if I would just melt into them. It made me uncomfortable, I wanted to move on.

"Sorry sir but I must take my leave and go to work."

"Yes you must, maybe I will see you sing later."

And with that, he walked off into the crowd of people with an air of confidence that made me feel distaste for him. Handsome as he may be, there was something that didn't sit well about his sudden appearance and strange confidence, though I didn't have time to ponder it; otherwise I would be late to work.

The rest of the morning went on with no more strange visits or interruptions until it was early afternoon and a much more cheerful visitor arrived. Annabel came in, she looked more rested but still moved slower than was usual for someone usually so lively. I offered to buy her a drink, but the look on her face was enough to tell me she had not fully recovered from last night's celebrations, even though she had no problem eating. We ordered. Every now and then I was called away to serve a customer, but our meal was relatively uninterrupted. We talked about the usual things that made up our conversations. Annabel liked someone at her part-time job, he had been invited out frequently to join us for drinking and dancing in the tavern, and I would spend my time reassuring her he liked her back.

After all, this much was true, he was a sweet boy but very shy, he still blushed when he spoke to her. When I tried to talk to him last night he only said how could he compete for a place in Annabel's heart when she had someone as beautiful and graceful as me in her life? I hoped he would get over that soon, for it was plain to see that when they were together their feelings were very much shared. After a little while, Annabel decided to change the subject.

"And what about you, Yue-ren? In all your time here I have yet to see you find someone. What I wouldn't give to see you gain that kind of happiness."

Even as she spoke, it was as if time stood still and all the room fell silent for he entered the bar. More handsome then any man I had seen, his hair shone woven gold, framing a face paler than most men, but not as fair as mine. He was dressed like an aristocrat; black thick hooded coat tailored and fitted which swayed about him as he walked to the bar. It was so heavy that it would have drowned an ordinary man, but he had a presence so strong that even a coat that shrouded him like the night sky didn't darken the intensity of his gaze and the magnificence of his stature. Then he turned to me, eyes looking straight into mine, piercing my soul; such focus, such passion. There was only one who had ever looked at me like that before, and at last, he was here, just a few strides away. I was barely aware that I had stood up; it felt like he was calling to me. I felt my body being drawn to him, but as I made the first step, I felt a pull on my arm.

"So Yue-ren, I finally know your type. You have good

taste but why don't you let me go over and introduce you, you don't want to seem too forward."

I wasn't sure how to explain to her that this was the man from my past, the only person I felt I could love, the one who had saved me and the one I had been waiting for. I placed a hand on her shoulder and just said, "It is him."

The look on her face said everything; she understood what made me act this way, why I felt so compelled not to waste another second.

Then it all changed, there was a shake and a sound like thunder, my world unhinged again.

There was a loud sound, it cracked and ripped through the air causing the windows to quiver; it was as if something had exploded, that made the very tavern shake bottles, rattling on shelves and plates danced and quivered. The silence I had been caught up in shattered like the glass windows as I quickly covered Annabel to stop the falling glass harming her. I heard screams outside. Before I had a chance to think, I was outside staring at a horrific sight. The factory chimneys were churning out a cloud of smoke much blacker than the evening sky, dusk was fogged over by a smoky night; one side of the building was nothing more than rubble, and a fierce fire was engulfing the rest. Flames of crimson ate away at the building, yellows and oranges, the brightest colours this city had seen grew like wild serpents.

The flames were reflected off the metallic surfaces casting an almost red tinge; a forbidding dusk colour like a blood sun was setting. I heard Annabel shout and start running towards the building, my heart sank and cold fear set into my bones, I knew Matthew would have been inside, and I suddenly realised that the furnace must have been faulty, he would not have escaped. Pure cold dread gripped me; I could feel the chill crawl done my spine like icy spiders walking across my skin.

My stomach churned, it felt like my insides were boiling and at the same time my blood ran cold, fear and rage and intense grief all swirling inside me, the urge to be sick as strong as the urge to cry.

And then my thoughts returned to Annabel, whatever emotions were gripping me must be tearing away at her.

I grabbed her arm, tried to hold her back; I felt the tears in my eyes spill down as I looked at her face, the picture of misery for she must have come to the same conclusion as I had. People were shouting all around, I managed to pick up bits of conversation, the fire trucks had been blocked by debris, they couldn't get close enough to put out the fires in the factory, and it was beginning to spread, then I heard someone shout.

"Annabel, Yue-ren! Your mother went there, she knows your father was working there, she and many others are trying to put out the fires by hand."

At that Annabel broke free and took off for the factory and I broke into a sprint after her, they were my family, I could not abandon them no matter who was waiting behind me. I ran, not looking back for fear it would distract me. I had to save them, not even he could keep me from that, he found me once, he would do so again. Still, I felt like I was being torn in two; one moment I was looking into the face of my dreams, my feet carrying me to my wildest fantasies and desires, and then the next my dreams had spun on an axis facing me towards nightmares. How could I have been so close to happiness only to be running towards despair?

If I could rip my heart and soul from my body, send ghosts of them in both directions to hold onto everything I would, but my mind was made up; I had a debt to pay, and for now, this was the right direction to be running in.

We ran towards the factory, the air itself was getting warmer. It was heavy and full of ash that got into my eyes. It was like a cloud of deep snow but in every way the opposite of snow, black and hot it sat in the air. The fires were getting worse, it had been a warm day and so bright, the breeze was able to spread them, and there was plenty to feed the flames. The area around the factory was darker; the black fumes were beginning to fill the sky and block even the early emerging starlight, it was like some scene from the Bible when something terrible was coming the sky would go dark. We reached the debris that was preventing the fire trucks from getting past as people tried to move it desperately while others clambered over it carrying water in buckets.

It looked so futile, without the truck people would never carry enough water to put out such violent flames, but nonetheless, Annabel climbed over it determined to find her parents in all the chaos.

Like so many, we scrambled over debris and when reaching the other side saw the real horror of it. At least a third of the building was destroyed, the rest in flames; no one could survive in there. Those who escaped were burnt beyond help, they would not survive, but still, people carried them to supposed safety. All around lay charred bodies thrown to the side from the blast. It was like the devil himself had broken free, bursting to the surface and destroying all in his path. The air was even hotter, and the smell of burning material filled the air.

I was covered with sweat, my hair matted and full of soot, but still I ran forward with Annabel in the hope we could be of some help.

We spotted Joy, her clothes and hair a mess, covered in soot and sweat as she tried to move the debris with bleeding palms.

"Joy, what are you doing, get away from there!"

I shouted in vain; she looked up for a second but then went back to desperately trying to pry apart bits of rubble.

"He is in there! I must get him out!"

I knew the look of pure desolation, like the debris, was crushing her very soul. She must have known that no one could have survived this, but still, she dug as if her life depended on it; frantic and desperate and muttering to herself again and again about how he was still in there. Annabel looked distraught and went to her mother's side where she had made a small entrance through the debris. I pleaded with her not to go in any further and that it was suicide, but she didn't listen, grief had consumed her senses, and her plight had affected Annabel too. I had no choice but to go into that burning tomb with them.

Inside was just as bad as outside; hot, dark, and heavy with that horrible smell and thick soot. If we weren't crushed by falling debris or burnt alive, we would die from inhaling this horrid air and smoke. It was strange how I had once saved Annabel from a frozen watery grave only to follow her into a hot, fiery one, such was the irony of life. We scrambled through the burning foundations till we came to the furnace room. It surprised me how we made it this far, it was unnaturally easy as if someone wanted us to get there to find something in this room. We did find something or should I say, someone.

Matthews's body lay not too far from us, burnt nearly to the point where we could only just about recognise him. His face looked like pain and anguish, the face of someone who would have been burnt in the fires of hell, it was horrible. I felt the tears flow freely, tried to rub them, only getting more of the horrendous soot and ash on my face. Joy was calm; in fact eerily quiet, like a spectre she moved slowly forwards not a tear in her eyes, a picture of serenity. She merely sat by her husband picking up his body and began to cradle him in her arms, rocking gently back and forth, comforting him.

The scene would have looked beautiful and peaceful had I been able to drown out the noise of the burning building. Annabel looked bewildered; her sobs were loud and clear as she took a step towards her parents.

"No dear, your father isn't well, I must care for him, why don't you go and get some fresh air. I'm sure he will be fine later he just needs some rest."

What a horrible thing, to lose your mind so quickly, she must have snapped the minute she realised her husband was dead and now she was going to sit there until she burned to death with him. A beam from above broke free, falling between us and all Annabel and I could do was watch as the two people I now called my parents slowly disappeared into a wall of flame. Annabel let out a piercing scream like no other, no longer being able to hold onto the grief; everything hitting her at once as she collapsed onto the ground in hysterical sobs, her whole body shook violently.

I wished my heart was still cold so that I could have looked at this from my closed-off world but I could not as I tried to get her up, tried to get us out of there.

"My dear Yue-ren you were my guardian angel, you saved my life and brought so much happiness to this family, but now it's all gone. You have to leave, get out of here, find the one you love, maybe live a happy life away from this mess."

Her words were soft and kind like many of our conversations, but I couldn't find anything to say back. Did she really think I would let her die here? I could not save our parents, but I had sworn once to protect her and nothing had changed. I tried to gather her up, but she fell limp, doing her best to make it nearly impossible to move her. I was determined I would save her, we would survive, so I drowned out all the sounds, blocked the smell, the heat and ignored the soot in my eyes and throat. Annabel looked at me; pure happiness gleamed in her eyes and genuine thankfulness.

"It was a pleasure knowing you, thank you but now it's time I returned the favour and save your life."

There was a crash, another beam broke free, and before I could pull us both to safety, she pushed me with all her strength out of its path as I watched it descend on her. It was my turn to scream at the sight of my first friend, the first person I really felt close to being taken away from me. From beneath the fallen mass, I saw her whisper to me; it was the last thing she said before she was gone, engulfed in flames, never to laugh, dance or talk again. Her last words were simple, "I love you."

Broken. I was broken.

I stumbled a bit but had no real reason to leave, even he was being forgotten, swallowed by grief, the one good flame in my life, the fire of love, desire and passion extinguished. It didn't stand a chance in this Hellstrom of blazing destruction as it simply vanished from me. I had nothing waiting out there for me; I just lost the only people who truly mattered to me. I allowed myself to sink to the floor, allowed every emotion I had to turn to smoke like the building around me as I vowed I would never let my heart to feel again. I was rejecting love in all its forms; I never wanted my heart to hurt this much again. That was my last thought as I drifted into unconsciousness and even though all around me flames burned, I felt myself go cold both inside and out until darkness claimed me.

————

I can't believe it; he was there, all my searching over, he was in front of me about to come to me, how could everything I hoped for be so near and yet so far?

I heard the explosion, I saw him run, and I knew that someone important to him must be in danger if he could just run without looking back, it hurt. I should have realised that in all this time he would have found someone, I saw the glow in his eyes as he talked to that girl; his heart was so much more open and loving now, how could there be a place in it for me? I decided to stay back, I didn't want to be in his way, I knew if I had gone after him, stopped him, he would never forgive me coming between him and those he now loved. After a while of standing there I noticed the sky around the factory where the explosion had taken place to grow dark, an omen if I ever saw one, a blood moon in play means foul deeds of supernatural consequence are in motion.

I ran, I had to make sure he was safe, that I could somehow prove myself and see for myself the people who had saved him. I had to know for sure if his heart truly belonged to them or if he had room for me.

That look in the bar, that recollection meant so much to me, it was as if he had been waiting for me. As I called to him, he had begun to move to me, I couldn't deny that he was waiting for me. Maybe the people he went to rescue were important in a different way. I hoped so much for that to be the truth. I felt no threat from the girl; he looked at her much like a brother would, so maybe he had found a family out here, and there was still room for the love I had for him. If I could help save them, prove this love for him, then all my desire would be realised and if I was wrong then maybe I could at least protect him from the flames and allow myself to perish. I knew my thoughts were going round in circles, it amazes me how this one human can cause a mind as sharp as mine to become so unrested.

Seeing him again in person had unsettled even my immortal soul causing conflicting feelings. Yet this is strange enough, years of waiting had made my lust and desire stronger but also that love, that very human feeling for so long I had been without. And this boy, no he was becoming a young man, he was letting me, love, and I was not a master of it, I was just as confused by it as any man. So I had to go forth and see this through, nothing was certain in this path, but I was ready to follow these feelings and see what happened when something so beyond human started to think like one.

But I arrived too late. Just as I came, I felt another presence leave, but it was not there long enough for me to recognise or truly determine what it was. I arrived to see the young girl use her last strength to push him to safety before everlasting darkness took her. I entered to watch the Yue-ren I'd once seen come back in all his coldness and renewed dark heart, his desolation returned, and he surrendered to nothingness. He slumped against the floor defeated, and I could only watch as he let the darkness creep in. I went to him, he was unconscious but alive, and I picked him up and walked out of there. A vampire has no fear of fire, it merely parted before me.

No one saw us leave; we merely disappeared into the night. I could feel his very soul grow cold and I knew of only one place to take him. I did not think he'd forgive me for returning him there, but it was somewhere I could watch over him, and at least it would be familiar to him.

I started our return to the opera house, where I would lay him to rest and await the man to rise from this desolate slumber, and I would wait to see what would come, to see what fate would befall my pure one's heart.

Chapter 10

Yue-ren.

WINTER DESCENDS UPON THE MOON

I HAD AWOKEN IN THIS PLACE AGAIN.

I should have known I'd never escape here; I was doomed to be a prisoner of my own body and home.

How selfish I had been, wanting to escape the life that had been given to me and become part of someone else's.

But I had lost it all; the family, friends and life I had made over the last few years, taken from me faster than I could imagine. The very fires of hell had eaten them, and I had been left alone again. I kept wondering what gave me the right to live? If anything, I deserved death so much more for the simple reason that I was jealous of them, jealous they were dead. I had to live on with their memories; it was I who had to face a world I hated in a body I hated. But what made me even guiltier, what made me ever more wretched was that I kept thinking how close I had been to him and now even that was gone. Even if he came to me now, I would not be able to look at him. I have lost all capacity to love. I'm empty and wish to live my days without any of my soul so I can forget everything I was and am. I want to be nothing more than a shell, let people look at my beauty let them hear my voice as I am nothing more than a puppet, a doll that doesn't live for myself but lives to make others' happy.

I will never love, laugh or feel again; I will just come and go until I finally can't anymore, and I waste away like a dying rose. I was made to be my mother's replacement in this world, and so be it, but I will not take comfort from anyone. I will give them their songs but I sing just because I can, it has no meaning here, just as I will remain a girl to them for there is no point trying to live for myself. I will merely be my mother's shadow as I always have, even his eyes can't look through me, I have nothing left inside for him, for he leaves me as cold as this world does, for I cannot and will not feel passion again. The fires of hell took the last of my love, the heat and warmth I had learnt from friends and a family gone, snuffed out like a candle in the breeze.

Without heat, without love, without passion, there is nothing to burn for, and thus I shall freeze. I have ice in my view, frost in my heart, my eyes shine like the surface of a frozen pool. I will be cold to everyone and even colder to touch so that I may have people recoil from me, afraid of the numbing sensation my body carries. Yes, I am frozen, a forgotten lake, a pool of despair and body of tundra. I will move like the frozen winds of the north, and when I can move no more, I will lie down like the fallen snow, waiting to be crushed beneath the feet of those who would enjoy me only to destroy me like snow by taking their pleasures from me.

I am broken from my thoughts by a tap at the door, how long had I been lying in my bed? I was vaguely aware that maids had put food on my table, which would lie untouched. No one had approached the bed I lay in; no one even looked at me apart from one. The one who put me here, secured my covers around me before departing from my side, the last bit of comfort in my life drifting away like a petal on the wind. The door opened, another maid walked quickly in observing the ignored food.

"Why do you bother to bring me this? I will not eat."

"You're awake! Sorry I didn't realise, please you must eat. You have been lying here for days; we thought you would never leave this bed."

She spoke nicely like you would to a child, but I soon lost interest in anything she said, rolling to my side whispering to her that I would not leave this bed unless I have to.

"But mam, he insists you eat, he comes every day with flowers for the opera house so that when you leave your room, you will be surrounded by beauty. What a handsome man, no one here could believe it when he carried you here. The governors want to hold a ball for you for when you recover, so you must leave this bedroom so you can dance with him."

She talked on like this, only half talking to me as I only half listened to her. I thought that an appearance by Yue-ren would calm rumour about my health, stop visitors coming to see if I was okay, but still, I knew in my heart, that cold wasteland, I had to see him. From the maid's description I knew who the man was that waited for me just outside these walls and I knew that I could use this ball to say goodbye to the last thing I had ever cared for in this life.

"I will eat; let the governors know that a party may lighten my spirits, let my fans know they have not lost their performer."

She left the room, I'm sure she didn't really understand my remark, but at least it got her out of here so I could get out of the bed. I sat by the dresser eating little from the plate of food, watching my pale reflection in the mirror. I was still beautiful, I admired the gentle curve of my neck to my delicate cheekbones that I once would have wanted to have felt feathery kisses, but now my skin feels cold. I run my finger over pink lips that will forever only know the kiss stolen from me so many years ago. My eyes sting, they want to cry but so withdrawn I have become that they will not spill. I am doomed to stay an innocent, loveless child, never to know passion, for I have lost too much to ever want to let myself be that liberated.

I go back to bed; I will wait to hear about the ball, society's pathetic attempt to proclaim self-importance and worship. If it weren't for the fact I wanted to say goodbye to him and maybe this world altogether, I would have faded right here and now.

By the end of that day, I had everything planned for the following night; the aristocrats didn't waste much time when it came to celebrating their self-indulgence.

This was meant to be my welcome back party, to celebrate the gift that was me. I knew it was really saying don't worry, our favourite toy has returned, we can make it sing and dance again or simply sit it so it can look pretty! What a horrid little world I had gone back to. This would be my farewell to them, to this stupid excuse of a life. I was tired of living, it was time to leave everything, I just needed to say goodbye to one person. I chose a dress, beautiful white silk that flows, ripples and pools at my feet; I feel like I am wearing liquid as the dress follows my every movement. Ivory coloured shoes, the type that can be easily danced in, and a large shawl about my shoulders to hide the flatness of my chest. I have only been back a short while but I can already remember the ways I used to hide myself, the female façade returns to me so easily. I leave my hair free, much like my mother did, my small tribute to her. Lipstick as red as blood coats my lips just to emphasise the harshness of my features, the striking paleness of my skin.

In front of this mirror stands the beautiful, graceful and elegant opera singer Yue-ren, every bit as loved as her mother. Satin gloves stop just before thin wrists with small delicate bracelets of silver. The moon has turned into liquid this night, and it has flooded this building with every step I take. How poetic my life seems; what a shame poetry is a wasted talent, much like my short life but for the next couple of hours I must at least appear part of this dreaded society. I leave my room, walk the cold halls of my prison to the grand ball that will act as my trial, be with the people that are my jury and say goodbye to the man that would have been my judge, for no matter what, tonight I feel will be my execution. I enter the room, gaze upon my world as people part and let me walk into the centre as if they want me for a spectacle, a centrepiece to look upon.

"Yue-ren you look as beautiful as ever, we worried so much about you. How was your trip abroad? Travelling must have been good, seeing the world, letting others enjoy your talents."

It was the owner of the opera house, he had taken over from his father, who had been a close friend of my mother and therefore kept my secret. But his son had not been informed; most of the small group that knew my secret was long dead or had left, everyone else believed I was a girl. I listened to him talk of my so-called travels, so a lie for my absence had already been created, how nice for everyone. Well, I suppose I should go along with it too, don't want to tarnish the reputation of the opera house by tales of its wondering stars, and anyway people seemed far more interested in how I was feeling or if I would sing later than where I had been. I talked to small groups, mainly talking to the other women about the latest fashions I had missed in my absence, how dull, acting in front of these people had become second nature. I could fool them into anything, if they all believed I was female, then it was easy to make them all think I was happy to be back.

After a little while, I began to hear stories of the area, strange accidents that turned into incidents of attackers and finally a young girl who had been found murdered, drained of blood, a real mess. I held near the gossipers enough to hear those attractive young aristocrats had been targeted for there was something foul at work in the city. It sounded like horror stories, these people were so far removed from the real world that the only tales of horror would have to be made up. They apparently had a new passion for these fantastical stories, unlike the story I held deep inside my memories, a true story that would have delighted them but was for me alone. All the victims had been young and attractive and drained of blood, the work of an escalating perpetrator.

"Miss Yue-ren be careful when you go out, especially at night, no doubt this person would love to get their hands on you."

For a brief second, it felt like somehow I knew she was right, that what she just said seemed true, but the thought was gone for he entered the room. The women around me began to blush and whisper around me all wanting to know who would dance with him. I remembered it like a dream, a distant feeling that time in the tavern but this time my heart didn't race. I knew how the women felt and why they blushed but it was all gone in me, that feeling had been buried, and part of me wanted it back just for a moment, just for tonight. But alas I knew that if I let him in my heart a little, the pain of losing him would be too high, I had to have a heart of stone. He walked over, calm and confident, eyes fixed on me, still that passion but also anxiety. Did he know what I was planning? Did he realise that after everything, I was planning on rejecting him?

"Would you do me the honour of one dance?"

He said it quietly, his voice as rich as chocolate, it would be a sin to indulge in it too much. I heard one of the other women say I didn't dance which was true, I hadn't danced in a very long time, but he was different; I owed him this much. I stretched out my hand gently and delicately, and he took it in his hand, healthy and confident like his strides to the dance floor. And for one moment, for one song, I forgot. The world faded out, everything moved slowly, it felt like I was floating, held tightly in his embrace. He was a graceful dancer with a steady stride, he held my hand tight but not enough to damage my wrists as the other arm wrapped around my waist, pulling me into him. I could feel the power of his body and rested my head against his chest, clinging to him as if I never wanted to let go; I wanted to be near him. He smelt musky, I could feel his breath on the back of my neck, his thumb caressing my back as we danced, and the passion from his gaze, the love.

All of a sudden I realised that I was about to fall, about to let my heart open and let this love in when I tried so hard not to. I couldn't look him in the eyes, I knew I would be lost, and then he whispered to me so only I could hear.

"Yue-ren, leave your mother's shadow, be the man you're supposed to and let me love you."

Chapter 11

Cain

THE SUN BREAKS OVER A FROZEN
MORNING

THIS FEELING WAS SO RELAXED, ALL MY ANGER WASHED away in every gentle stride and movement we made across the dance floor.

Holding him close to me, feeling his body against mine, we moved as if one, as if it was meant to be.

For the first time, I felt complete and alive; I had the one I loved above all else in my embrace. I had many things to say; I did not want to scare him or reveal his secrets to the people around us. I had to do this with care; I could see the looks from other people at this ball, could already imagine the gossip, didn't want anything to hurt the creature within my arms. I still had many secrets to tell him, apprehension about what he would think of my true nature, would he accept me? I had come so far, I was too close to let myself slip now, I was resolved that tonight I would have my answer. I would either have the one I love in my arms, or it would be in the arms of the one I love I would die.

So finally I have revealed myself, every desire on the verge of being fulfilled even my lust for him would not cloud my thoughts of how this scene should be played out.

I whispered to him one thing I waited for many years to say, my façade of confidence not withering at the risk of expressing my feelings for a man I had spent so long reaching for. In a fraction of time, a moment of space, a pause of reality, it began and ended with four words, "let me love you." As quickly as my freedom had seemed possible, my desire fulfilled, an obstacle appeared. As I relaxed from the whispered confession, Yue-ren's body tensed. He pushed away not even meeting my eyes, released his hold of me and excused himself. At first, he walked across the dance floor now filled with silent whispers and then vanished into the dark corridor. I would not have seen him if not for my vampire's eyesight, but once out of mortal view, he quickened his pace to a run.

I felt my heart tighten, denied with no conclusion, my hands balled into fists as I strode with confidence from the ballroom to give chase.

Once in the cold dark corridors, I knew that no one would follow; why would they get involved when they could continue their party, their false celebration. I also knew that Yue-ren was not so far in front of me, I could hear his breath, panting as he ran down the halls, all I needed to do was use the powers that came with my true nature, and I would be before him. So in a cloud of dust I dissipated, I knew this may scare him, but I had too strong a passion and perseverance to stop now.

Like fog gliding over the surface of the water I travelled to find Yue-ren standing by a balcony looking out into the night, clouds beginning to obscure some of the sky, thick and dark, but part of the moon still shone through. Like a painting, he stood bathed in moonlight. His hair licked his cheeks as one hand brushed away the dancing strands, his breath was still not even from the run, and I could see it against the cold night. But like the night he stood cold, motionless, not an emotion in those alabaster features, he was indeed like a statue. You could have compared him to one of those beautiful Greek statues of ancient times that depicted the most beloved of gods and goddesses, such a distant and untouchable beauty doomed to stay frozen in the form of stone.

I appeared before him, watched his eyes widen as smoke turned to form and amber eyes glowed as bright as the moonlight. He regained his composure trying not to let an emotion escape as he took a step back from me; I could see concealed fear behind that cold exterior. What had happened to my precious one's soul? Where had it gone? All I saw was fear but nothing else; it was all masked, if not worse, it was buried and forgotten. His lips parted as if to speak but no sound came out, the question I knew I would have to answer hanging from his mouth. So I talked to try and break the silence that engulfed us.

"My name is Cain; I waited until now to come to you for fear of what my true nature would do to you. I watched you grow into such a beauty but did not know how you would accept me as a man. I am a creature of the night, the stuff of legend, one of the rumours, but it was all done to protect you. I appear now for I can no longer stay away."

Still no words, just quiet acceptance, it was eerie the calm he held like I was indeed talking to an inanimate form, making a confession to an empty vessel. I had to try and break him, release the emotions beneath the surface for his sake as well as mine, we both needed a release.

"Yue-ren I know all your secrets, I read your letters and I have watched you and longed for you. I love you for everything, and I cannot deny my passion and desire for you, but it is for the real you. I can bring you happiness, allow me to save you. Let me love you."

I felt my passion; it burned in every fibre of my body. I

wanted to grab him, to kiss him, to prove just how much my love burned for him. He was slumped against a wall, broken he looked and yet so beautiful. If I had not waited for this moment for so long, if I had not prayed so hard to whatever force may allow us to be together, I would have taken him here and now. I would have dragged him to the ground and devoured him, releasing all pent up lust and intense emotions.

I would have filled him with my passion until he could no longer resist, till he cried for me to engulf him until his own desire was released. I wanted to see him consumed with heat till his icy exterior melted and his soul lived, and I wanted above all else for him to beckon me to do it. A single tear rolled down his perfect face leaving a glistening trail down a pale check. He drew his arms around himself as if afraid something was about to escape and then our eyes met.

"How dare you come to me now, like this, now I am nothing but an empty shell? You watched me wither and die, praying for a release, where was your passion then? I don't need your love, I don't want it. Do you think I'm stupid? I know what you'll offer me, but I waited for so long for you, and you never came, and now I'm beyond any chance for a new life. Do you think I want some undying creature telling me he understands my pain? Yes, I know what you are."

Tears flowed freely, staining his cheeks, causing his make-up to run; his words were becoming increasingly hard to make out between the sobs. Each one pierced me like a stake to the heart, and yet he continued.

"Isn't this where you offer me eternal life and beauty so I can become your plaything for all eternity? Well, I'm sorry, I won't play this game, I've been hurt too much. I can't handle this and I won't."

He broke into a run, desperate to get away from me he fled towards the stairs. I was in shock, I never realised how much pain my absence had caused him; I thought I was protecting him. It wasn't my true nature he feared, it was me, it was my selfishness at not being able to confront him with these feelings I had had all along. He had waited for me for as long as I had watched him; from that encounter in the rain he had expected for me to save him, yet I never came. He wasn't hurt to learn that the one he loved was a creature of the night; he was troubled that the one he loved never came to save him until it was too late.

Too late, I played the words in my head, no it wasn't too late. I had lived so long that I forgot mortals didn't have the same patience I had developed, but I was going to convince him that there was still something to save, not to destroy all these feelings before we even tried to resolve this.

I gave chase. Outside, as if in some bad movie, the weather had changed, the pale moon obscured by clouds that began to spill their contents. How appropriate, a confrontation in the rain. Out into the open air, I burst, rain dropping down on me and the view before me. Yue-ren stood on the rail of the balcony, all he needed to do was let go, and my entire existence would mean nothing. His dress ruined by the falling rain, soaking him through till clothes and hair clung to his distraught form.

"I can't do this anymore; live a life of unfulfilled prayers and dreams, I don't care anymore. I have been lost in the dark, and I don't ever want to escape. You could have anyone, you can do anything, why settle for a lost soul, a useless wretch of a man living in an inescapable shadow? How could you feel passion for one who should have fallen into an icy grave long ago? Maybe if things were different, I could have accepted you, but the way I am now, all I can do is free you from the curse, that is my pointless existence."

I knew that look, he wanted the same release I did, he felt unworthy of love, he thought that his end would mean my escape from him. If only he knew that I was the one unworthy of him. I wanted to release him from me, how could things have gone so wrong? In a second he let go, spilling back into the night falling like the rain itself. For the second time, that evening time slowed as I watch him slip from view, lost to the inevitable darkness. Is this how it was destined to end?

Was it really too late for us, doomed before we even tried? No, I refused; I had grown weak from my own insecurities but not anymore. This mortal, this man who owned my soul, I had to have the strength for both of us. I grabbed his hand, his body swinging dangerously but my grip was firm, I was relentless.

"Idiot, do you think I would come all this way to let you destroy yourself? I haven't watched, desired and obsessed over you this long to let you leave me. I will show you what love can do, I can save you still. I will not be denied the only thing I have ever craved beyond any other desire."

With that I hoisted him over the balcony, shock apparent in his face; at least his emotions were there, on the surface for me to read. He struggled against my hold, but I pulled him into me, tightening the embrace I had on his body and closing my lips on his. The contact was dangerous; he resisted at first, but I would not let go until I felt his defence weaken. The violent crush of lips became soft; his hands that were balled into my clothes relaxed and fell to his sides. His body gave in as my harsh hold of his shoulders loosened, and I wrapped my arms around his waist pulling him into the kiss.

His lips parted allowing me entrance as I deepened the kiss, his hand searched for a place to rest as they knotted in my hair pulling himself to me, seeking desperately for that feeling he had longed for, passion; it burned between us as the rain continued to soak us, but what did we care? We had found something we had both been looking for; a deep yearning had been fulfilled. Time went on, for ages it seemed, we were locked into the passionate embrace until he needed to withdraw for air.

His eyes, full of sadness like the realisation of how stupid he acted, shone at me from behind his curtain of snow like hair. There was a deep blush on his cheeks, and a small smile played on his lips, a sad smile like this feeling was about to disappear. He buried his head into my chest; I knew he was crying again, but this time I would be able to soothe those tears away; I would prove this was no dream and that I was here to stay, to heal his wounded soul. I picked him up into my arms like that day so long ago, but this time I kept my eyes fixed on him so he knew I was there, that he wouldn't go to sleep and find me gone. We walked back into the building walking towards a new destiny, a chance for a pure life; I had the one I loved in my arms, nothing would let him leave those arms.

I would never jeopardise that; I would live for him and him alone from now on.

Chapter 12

Laphel

THE GAMES OF A MALICIOUS STORM

Stupid, disgusting creature!

How dare it touch what is mine?

It thinks it shall get away with tainting that what belongs to me. If I had known that very creature I had met one night in a bar not so very long ago was after the same prize, I would have altered this plan. It made me sick to think of his lips on what I should be tasting.

I knew Yue-ren would have escaped the fire, it was supposed to play out like that, watch his beloved family and life engulfed by the very fires of hell it would appear. I should have stayed that little bit longer to stop him from interfering. I had not foreseen this and that vampire had made me seem foolish, me a demon. But this was more than hurting my pride; he has taken something that did not belong to him.

The plan was that the fire fighters would find Yue-ren before any physical harm came to him but leaving such emotional scars that his soul would be lost and I could claim his body. However he did not appear in the hospital like I thought and soon I heard his body had never been found.

I felt in my blood that he was still alive; there was only one place he could be; he had returned to the world before, the place that haunted him so. At first it seemed like things had worked out; he was back in the place that caused him so much pain and despair. And when I caught up with him his soul was indeed lost, buried by such sorrow. He was so beautiful like that, a broken doll begging me to play with it. Then he entered that scene. I listened and followed that night of the ball how this handsome stranger had brought Yue-ren home. A vampire that loved a mortal, it never worked, one would always reject the other so I thought this would only strengthen the loss in Yue-ren's soul.

I let them dance, have their moment and then followed them becoming drunk on Yue-ren's own words of bitterness and refusal. I had never thought how much pain it would cause, how I smelt the desire of that vampire, he was using all his control and it brought him nothing.

Up until that scene on the balcony everything was going so nicely; Yue-ren would take his life willingly and his eternal soul would be mine to torture for all eternity. It was sooner than I'd plan for his beautiful death, but at least that vampire would not get his claws on him. Their scene was so overpowered by emotion that neither one noticed another presence hiding among the stone creatures that decorated the roof ledge above them. So close, so very nearly all mine. Yue-ren was so lost, there was no return for him, save for that foul creatures embrace.

It took every inch of will for me not to rip them apart there and then. I knew I could not fight a vampire lord at night, I had to calculate my revenge but still it burned so bright this hatred in me. Disgusting creature, violating what was mine alone to violate. He was treating my possession with care, love, devotion and passion, reawakening his soul.

They were both so alive they felt saved, all my hard work and plans ruined over one kiss.

I had to destroy this emotion in them before it grew strong enough to take my pretty boy from me.

I was lucky that my precious toy was so drained from the release of emotion that he had been left to sleep before that creature could truly claim him, what a gentleman this vampire was. He left his sleeping love alone as he walked the hall to find a dark corner to think; no matter how happy he may be, a vampire still needs time alone to brood over their thoughts and this is all the time a demon needs to play his little games. I appeared in my little doll's room wearing the form of the one creature I knew he wouldn't refuse.

"Wake up my sleeping beauty."

I placed a soft kiss on his temple and was greeted by pure blue eyes, how innocent and lovely he looked.

He was about to answer me but I silenced him with a kiss, so yielding in my grasp, how easy it will be for me to take him. I pushed him into the bed, hands stroked smooth flesh as I watched pale cheeks turn pink. I began to remove his sheets from about him, he lay there exposed to me not an inch of fabric on him as I pinned him to the bed with my body.

"Please Cain, I'm not ready, I'm not sure I can do this yet."

"Don't worry my pretty boy, I'll make you ready."

The words sparked something in him; his eyes opened with sudden fear like some panicked realisation. He tried to push me off but I used my arms to pin his so he could not escape me. I continued to torture him with soft kisses, turning to little nips at his skin. I could feel his body tremble as he tried to resist, but this was my will, I had to mark him as mine, I would not yield.

Beside the little noises he made only helped to fuel my

growing desire as I forced more weight onto him kissing him violently till I could taste his sweet blood on my lips. He looked at me, fear in his gaze, as I watched a small trail of blood, nothing more than a droplet run down his chin.

"How beautiful you look stained in blood, my precious little boy."

Wordlessly he tried to ask me to stop, tears spilling from his eyes.

"You think I'd let that vampire be the first to claim you, don't you know you're mine? Don't worry; I'll make you feel good, just like your mother. Oh how much she moaned under my touches, she could never get enough of me."

I smiled at him my grip on his arms, a demon's touch can burn through fabric if so desired and I was tempted to burn a mark into his white skin. Our eyes met and then in a second he used a strength I never realised he had.

"Your eyes, they're not the same, I can't see the passion I normally see, you're not Cain! Let me go, don't touch me! Cain help me!"

So, the boy had some fight in him. His sudden burst of emotion had caught me off guard long enough for me to release my hold of his arms. He pushed himself away from me gathering his bedding about him to hide his obvious shame.

"Poor boy, if only you had let yourself believe I was your un-dead lover you could have enjoyed this but now I will have to take you by force."

I lashed out grabbing hold of his beautiful hair like satin in my fingers, dragging him to the floor. He shouted but I silenced him again with another violent kiss, tears evident and then he was still.

Lifeless, he lay there apart from small breaths. His body went limp beneath me, no resistance at all. I did not like this; it was one thing to force myself on him, take him by force and have him resist, that would have been so much fun. But now it would be like making love to someone asleep or dead and there was no pleasure in that.

"You are no fun today my boy, maybe I should go play with your other half and let you wallow in your own self pity, but if that vampire even tries to touch you, I will not hold back. Next time I will make your body mine with such force you'll never allow anyone to touch it again."

With a smile I left him there on the floor, bruised and sobbing, so attractive he was like this it amazed me how I could resist.

I listened happily to the muffled sound of light sobbing as I walked away from his room, it made me want to hum a tune the joy it gave me. As the sound became softer and faded out it was instead replaced with that smell of dark emotion. A scent carried in the air that only a demon could smell, a scent almost pungent enough to taste. Yes, there it was; the divine flavour of lust, it was aged like good wine, this smelled of fortified lust, rich and dark. An old vampire was this creature, but proof that even the old and wise become weak to emotions such as love.

My footfall was silent on the wooden floor, not a squeak of a floor board as I wound down the corridor. I gave a little nod to a portrait of Selena; after all, she was a great beauty and deserved that much. If I had not wanted to go torture this dark offender I would have stopped to give thanks to Selena-Ren for being such a deliciously sinful woman and be the one to help realise my own wishes but alas I had bigger plans now.

I walked the halls to a dark room, some kind of private smoking room where this vampire Cain stood, back to the door, helping himself to a glass of wine. I changed my form to the beautiful creature I had just left; let's see what I could do to this creature. I walked in and immediately he turned to face me. I noticed those amber eyes so filled with passion and desire, no wonder Yue-ren had seen through mine, they could never have that intense look of love. But it was that love that made this Cain creature weak, as he now had a weakness for a demon to prey upon.

I walked up to him and as I approached he extended an arm to pull me into his embrace and plant a kiss upon my lips, but I turned my head, resisting his kiss and noted the look of confusion in his face. Ah, poor vampire, not used to rejection. I turned my stare cold and pushed out of his arms. His confusion could be read all through his body as he tensed with the lack of contact with his one true desire.

"Do you think I would enjoy being with you? It was a fool's hope, I knew you could save me, I simply tested you out there on the balcony, but now I have had time to think I realise I don't want a creature like you as a lover. Do you think I would enjoy making love with a corpse? Your touches are like poison to me, I feel sick at the sight of you."

If he felt hurt he hid it well but I could see him tense, his hands rolled into balls, his fingernails digging into his palms, a thin line of blood had been drawn as it began to drip onto the carpet.

I had hurt him.

The victory ended all too soon as his fist loosened and his features grew dark, his eyes cold and dangerous.

"Put your spiteful tongue back in your mouth, Demon."

"So you figured it out, took a little while didn't it vampire? Has love for a human clouded your mind, fogged your senses, blinded your eyes? Poor creature, how far you have fallen."

Still that cold stare, I knew I was overstepping many boundaries but I had to make him pay no matter what he said.

"Shut up, be gone from me, you have nothing to say to me."

"No, Mr Lord of the Night, you will listen to me, I have much to say to you. Yue-ren is mine! I have watched his life from before he had life, he was destined to me and I won't let you have him."

"It seems we have the same love; who knew we shared such tastes?"

He looked so smug and sure of himself but I will see him broken yet.

"Yue-ren is free to choose his own life you have no hold on him."

"No. You are sadly mistaken, Yue-ren belongs to me, and he carries my mark. So clouded by your own obsession for him you have failed to notice whose mark he carries. Just like his mother, I will own his soul. After all, it's in his blood."

That vampire just stood there watching me, waiting for an explanation and I was not going to deny him that, I would win this little battle.

"Don't look so shocked it's unbecoming of a vampire. Why don't you do as your true nature dictates and taste him, blood doesn't lie. Know the truth from what your obsession was spawned and where he will return."

Those were my last words and it was all I needed, he understood what I had told him.

He backed away, using an arm to steady himself on the counter, he looked quite sick. I didn't stay long enough to read his emotions; let him deal with this information alone, I had had my fun, it was his turn to decide what to do.

I left the room and made my way out of the opera house; I would return in a bit to see how the rest of this performance played out, what fun I was having.

Chapter 13

Yue-ren

CAN THE MOON NEVER KNOW WARMTH?

THE FLOOR WAS COLD, THE ROOM WAS COLD, MY ENTIRE body was cold.

I assumed this is what a corpse would feel like on a morgue table. Unfortunately, I was still alive. Lost in my own thoughts, I didn't want to come back to such harsh reality and face what had just occurred. I just lay there, bathed in the early morning sunrise's light. My pale form glowed a golden sheen that made the marks on my body even more visible to my own eye. My wrists were bruised; I could feel the dull pain in them threatening to make me realise how close I had been to having the fate I had barely escaped once. Too soon my mind focused, he would have raped me had I not been so submissive.

I felt sick to the very pit of my stomach, my scalp hurt from the residual feeling of having my hair pulled, I wanted to cut out every strand that had been touched, but that meant getting up and facing my reflection in the mirror and I didn't want to look at myself. Last time I had been threatened like this Cain had saved me, but this time it had been

Cain or something that looked like Cain that had attacked me.

That was the most painful part, he said he had done the same to my mother, and she had enjoyed it. Cain had confessed to being a vampire and if such a creature existed then what other beings of legends and darkness walked this world? What was this thing that wore Cain's face, was it also a vampire or something else entirely? Too caught up in my own quest to find someone to love me I had put to the back of my mind Cain's true nature. A vampire; how quickly I had accepted that without truly understanding what it meant, I was just glad to be loved.

A vampire never dies, they live forever, I had no idea how old Cain was, what exactly his form of love would entail. This thing that was Cain but not was it old like him? Would it have had previous lovers my mother included?

Did Cain also have previous lovers and could my mother have been one? Either could have also been with my mother long before me. Did Cain only claim to love me, as a replacement for her? Was I again being forced into her shadow? It was too painful to bear the idea, was he trying to confuse me, to break me so he could have his way with me? Was I nothing more than a new toy for this other being? It would indeed explain his behaviour. Lull me into a false sense of hope and security until my guard was down then turn on me. I had come to know so much sorrow, it was twisting in my gut like a tapeworm, eating my positive thoughts of Cain with the poisonous ones this imposter made me feel. There was a doubt, a fear that wasn't there before, my own insecurity allowing me to entertain the idea that maybe it was Cain all along. I shook my head, I couldn't believe that, something else was at work trying to confuse and corrupt me.

But if it was indeed Cain that had left me just now, why

did his eyes not shine the same? Why did they not hold that light I had fallen in love with?

Maybe this was Cain's true nature, perhaps he could not control his lust for me and that lead to the sudden outburst, maybe I should have let him take me? Slowly I pulled myself from the floor, no it had not been Cain but why didn't he come save me? I dragged myself to my feet and was greeted by the reflection in the mirror. My lips were swollen, and they hurt to touch, the sting of a single fingertip. The trail of blood on my chin had dried; a crimson tear stained my face along with the trace of tears across my cheeks.

My eyes were red and bloodshot; I looked like some horrid ghost, so white with horrible red eyes staring back at me. I was indeed bruised; I cursed my body for being so fragile and having no shame, to show me the scars of my own defeat. A bruise on my hip where his hand had held me, one on my shoulder blade from the impact with the floor and of course restraint marks on my thin wrists.

I had to know whether I had only chosen more misery by finding an un-dead lover for company. I refused to believe that Cain was the one who had attacked me but who had it been, and what would Cain think if he knew how easily I had given in? Would he be ashamed to look at me? But if there was another out there that indeed wanted me, that meant Cain had a rival, a rival that could hold the face of the one I truly wanted to be with. I was being torn in two; I wanted to see Cain, my Cain, but what if the one that attacked me was the true inner nature of Cain. And as much as I tried to think otherwise, how could I trust that the Cain I met would not be some other in disguise trying to seduce me, or worse, make good on his promise to own me. Lastly, if there were indeed two creatures that desired me, I only wanted to be with Cain himself, how could I face him knowing I had let another touch me?

I grabbed the sheet that had fallen by my side to wrap my aching body in, no matter what I faced, rejection, domination or understanding I had to face Cain. I could not bring myself to change, instead of hiding my shame and self in the white sheet. Even the maids would not confront me like this; they let me walk by just nodding their "good morning ma'am's" as they busied themselves. I could have been a ghost to them, the white sheet phantom that ran down the halls of the opera house. My body was tired, and my head hurt from too many thoughts as I stumbled down the corridors. There was one room I knew I would find him in, a small smoking room. It had large wooden shutters which unless specially asked for, they would not be opened. It was a dark room that was lit by candles, and it seemed the kind of place a vampire would dwell in happily. I was lucky I had good instincts for there he was but not like I expected to find him.

He was slumped in a chair, his blonde hair fell forward obscuring half his face as the other half was buried in his hand. His arm was draped over the chair's arm, a wine glass sat dangerously in hand about to fall at any moment.

"Cain?"

I whispered it softly, not failing to hear the hushed pleading tone in the word. As soon as his name passed my lips the glass fell from his hand, breaking the silence within the room. I noticed the now empty palm looked red as if it had been cut. It seemed to be healing and indeed as I watched the red slowly became paler until there was no mark and I believed I had imagined it. His eyes looked up to me, and I was afraid to look at them, so much doubt was in me. There was confusion in them, searching as well as if he was unsure that it was really me that stood before him.

Then realisation as that look grew more convinced and passion that came with his gaze filled them.

I tried to take a step forward but I was shaking, and the sheet had begun to unwind from my trembling form. I was revealing myself to him, a silent question to him; will you reject or take me? He looked so unsure that I could not take that longing in his gaze, he was controlling himself, and I knew for sure that it had not been him in my room. His eyes glanced over my body, I could feel him taking in every view, and then his view rested on the bruise on my hip and his brow knitted together.

The shame, I felt ashamed to be there offering myself to him when it was apparent I'd let another touch me. I wasn't entirely sure what I wanted, but fear of rejection settled like a thick mist. I broke, feeling my knees strike the floor as my body gave in. I wrapped my arms around myself to steady my shaking form as I hunched over to hide my face from his view so he wouldn't see my tears. How weak he must think I am! I realised that the bruise on my shoulder blade would be in full view, what a disgrace I must be, I felt dirty.

"I'm sorry, I thought it was you when I realised it was not I tried to fight, I tried, I… "

I knew he would think the worst and I was trying so hard to get the words out but my throat felt so constricted.

"I gave in, I am so weak and disgusting, I stopped fighting it, and it didn't want me anymore, but I didn't know what to do. I was scared, unable to fight back."

I felt a soft hand on my shoulder, a gentle kiss on my cheek and then my ear.

"Do not worry my love, I know what it is, and I shall not let it have you."

Those words were warm and comforting, holding an understanding I did not think possible. I wanted to fall into his embrace so much. I raised my head looking up into to his face; I wanted to kiss him, I wanted to erase the kiss of whatever creature had tried to use me. As he leant in to claim my lips in a sweet embrace I yearned for, I panicked. I pushed away from him, every warning bell ringing, my entire body tensed.

All I could think of was that creature's kiss; it had taken my precious memory and destroyed it, warping the one thing I was holding onto in this world.

"I'm sorry I can't, I'm not ready, forgive me but I need time to forget this day. Please don't leave me and I promise when I'm ready I'll be yours."

Hurt crossed his features but also understanding as he withdrew from me.

"Come, let me escort you to your room, you can't walk down a corridor in nothing but a sheet."

He placed his jacket over me, a sad smile on his lips.

"I waited this long to be with you, I can wait a bit longer."

If I did not know better, I would think it was rejection, I sensed in his voice and coldness in his eyes. We walked the halls to my room; it took a little longer, but these were passages without windows to let light in that may harm him. The opera house was more alive now, and I could see the maids and other guest look at us. They all whispered, I could hear them, 'Yue-ren has a lover', but it felt more like I had just lost one. By pushing away from Cain, I had lost a small amount of his warmth and love that I hoped I would regain. I did love him, but I was not ready to accept his love, not with the very image of him trying to break me so strongly in my mind.

The closer we got to my room the more fear grew within me as I realised the image that was conjured up in my mind. I was bringing Cain back to the place where someone or something that looked just like Cain had left me.

I entered the room closing the shutters before letting Cain in, and I turned to him to see anger taint his handsome features. Was it anger at me for being so submissive, was it anger at himself for not hearing my calls and coming to my aid or was it anger at whatever had tried to take me here?

"Gather your things Yue-ren, you should stay in another room for now. This place must create bad memories and images I feel harmful to you and to me."

The last two words were said quietly as if he was unsure he wanted me to hear them but I indeed gathered some clothes. He turned away so I could dress without his gaze upon my body, how selfish I felt. Then we left the room, Cain asked a maid to tidy it and make up another guest room for me to stay in. She quickly disappeared ahead of us to air out an unused guest room but by request promptly shut the windows and curtains upon our arrival. We were soon left alone, my heart beating for I knew that Cain would leave me alone and I didn't want that. I clung to his arm like a child afraid of the dark, but when he reached for me, I felt myself flinch again.

"When you know what you want. I'll be by your side, for now, rest, I will watch over you from afar like I have always done."

As if to make sure I knew what he was and will always be he disappeared into a cloud of smoke before being gone from view altogether. I couldn't even begin to trace where he might have gone, but I felt his presence diminish, and I was left alone. I lay on the unused bed, alone again and so cold.

The bed was cold, the room was cold, and I was cold both inside and out. I had to find out for sure, I had to make sure this lack of warmth was not my fate.

Chapter 14

Cain

THE SPITEFUL RAIN

THE OPERA HOUSE WAS SILENT, YOU COULD HEAR nothing but the housemaids tiding up rooms and making the place look presentable for those who came and went.

With this building being such a draw for aristocrats whether there was a performance or not it had to be well looked after. The doors were always opened, and the opera owner always made sure it was clean and tidy to keeps its wealthy guests coming. It was good pay for the maids and cooks that dwelled here; they also got accommodation in the lower parts of the building away from, the more wealthy inhabitants. The opera house was lived in by only a small group of nobles. One main occupant was its current owner, the young Peter Arlington, and some of his friends. Of course, the primary occupant of this building, although she never much appeared at social events, was Yue-ren. But now there had been another dwelling within the opera house. There was now an exquisite gentleman with long blond hair and a manner that dripped with power and sensuality. His very presence was beginning to make quite a stir, not only for the aristocrats but the workers, especially the young maids, one maid in particular.

Lillian Underwood was a maid like many young women who had come to the city to find work and better themselves. She had been overjoyed when she learnt that she would be working at the opera house for the great talent Yue-ren. A graceful girl, who presented herself in such a manner you would think she thought herself above her own class. But Lillian was unique not only in appearance, with bright green eyes and curly red hair that was only ever half tied back. She had something that made her more dangerous, and that was ambition. Not just satisfied with having a job, money and a comfortable place to live, she wanted more, much more. She had tried to escape the life of a maid, but those aristocrats that had spoken of love and taking her into their society had never held true. They had merely wanted her body, as a relationship with a maid could be severed faster than with a woman of nobility and riches, but then Lillian had only slept with them in the hopes of getting their money.

Now there was a difference, Lillian Underwood had a goal, something she wanted more than money. She had set her sights on a certain gentleman and was determined to steal him away from his current interest. As she figured it; she had much more to offer than that shy, reclusive and frigid Yue-ren.

"I still can't believe a gentleman of such distinction could seriously settle for someone like the lady Yue-ren, I mean she is every bit as beautiful as they all say, but still her personality is somewhat lacking."

Lillian made herself clear.

"Careful what you say, Lil if the nobles find you speaking about the lady like this you'll be out of here. I can't see why you're not satisfied with life here; I mean we get treated good, with good pay and somewhere good to sleep. So what does it matter if the lady Yue-ren is a little reclusive? She lets us be, you can't complain about that." Another of the maids reprimanded.

"A little reclusive? I'd say a little nuts. She spends day after day locked in her room and then she disappeared for years! Comes back and nobody bothers to find out where she has been, so life goes on the same."

"She was away on business."

"If you believe that, you'll believe anything. I think she lost it and ran off. If her new gentleman had not brought her back, she would have stayed lost. I still can't believe her luck; she goes mad and then gets saved by the most handsome man I've ever seen. If you ask me, I think she seduced him and made him bring her back. The poor guy probably doesn't leave her side because she has some hold on him."

The other maids had gathered to hear Lillian speak, most of them had become aware of her dislike for the lady Yue-ren, but more apparent was her feelings towards the handsome gentleman that now walked the corridors. The other maids had given up trying to ask Lillian, or Lil as they called her, to stop speaking so out of line but Lil had strength and passion they did not, and it frightened them, this determination she had.

"You know what, even though I wasn't here at the time, I think that Selena-ren probably committed suicide because she couldn't handle Yue-ren taking her life from her. I bet the daughter was stealing her men, fame and fortunes, living off what her mother worked for until poor Lady Selena couldn't handle it any more. Even worse, maybe Yue-ren killed her mother to finally get rid of the competition, and the guilt is why she acts so strange."

"Lil, don't speak such things, go back to work my dear, I think this conversation has gone on long enough."

The elder maid ushered the others to follow suit and go back to their chores, allowing Lillian to speak on the subject no more. The corridor they had gathered in began to empty, and soon Lillian was left alone to continue the dusting of old portraits that lined the walls. Housework was really all for show, it made the aristocrats feel even more rich and snobbish if they had maids and butlers about. Underneath the opera and its Victorian façade was modern technology. Cookers, washers and dryers all making the need for maids pointless, all they had to do was load and push a button, technology did the rest.

But the rich were all about show and the outside appearance, so they liked the sight of maids using old cleaning utensils like dusters, and they insisted that all great feasts were handmade. A maid's life was more like that of an actress playing the part of a maid in the aristocrats' playhouse.

Lillian knew her role well, but sometimes she laughed at these stupid people with more money than sense. Time passed with only her own thoughts to keep her company, and soon the inner monologue was running.

"Lucky I should be able to work here for a woman who is clearly not altogether there in mind. The gentleman Cain; what he needs is a real woman, someone who has some life in her. The others don't understand at all, I mean they can't even grasp the situations I discuss with them. In fact, they can't even grasp my name! I have given up telling them to call me Lillian, I hate Lil. I wonder how many of them know my real name anyway, what do they think Lil is short for? But Cain, I see the great wisdom that comes with him, he would understand me. Such a handsome man I have never seen, such passion is hiding just beneath the surface, and I can give it to him, I know I can. I could spend hours just thinking about the man, daydreaming of what it would be like to kiss him or have him make love to me."

By now I have lost all desire to work, I am lost in my own fantasy world where Cain is mine, and I belonged to him.

A world where there is no Yue-ren or opera house with its half-wit maids and aristocrats alike. I wandered the corridors until I came upon the stairs that lead to the upper levels where Yue-ren dwells. More importantly, this is also where Cain would be found, as a dying need to see him; if only a glance, came upon me. Up the stairs I crept into the corridors, I had last seen either of them when they had asked for Yue-ren's room to be changed, and I had been the one to air out the guest quarters for them. When I had last seen them together, there had been tension in the air, and something was not right with the couple. If I wanted to take Cain for myself, this would be the time to do it as there was something amiss between the couple. The room that Yue-ren now dwelled in was closed from public view, and as I pressed my ear to the door, not a sound echoed within.

A little further down was a study, the kind of small comfortable room Cain liked to dwell in. The door was ajar, the light on inside but not a sound escaped. I pushed the door not expecting to see anyone inside since there had been no sound. Instead, I was greeted by the very view I had so wished upon seeing. He was there in all glory and yet something was different, hunger in his eyes I had not seen before.

"I'm sorry my lord, I did not realise you were here."

I bowed, letting my red hair fall forward and smiled. He was unmoved and yet his eyes looked almost carnal. It was as if he was desperate to devour something but was holding back.

The room felt hot, and Cain looked like an animal, a

wild beast that had been tortured by its keepers and was ready to pounce on the next person who would dare touch it. Of course, it was perfect, Yue-ren must not be allowing her new lover any of the release he obviously needed, and I had always known she would have been the frigid type. And now here was I, so ready to offer that release to a man that looked more like a caged lion, he needed me. I began to step closer, a look held in my features that offered comfort.

"My Lord are you okay? You look hungry, should I fetch you some food from the kitchens?"

"No, it is of no concern, please leave me be, you should return to your work."

His words came out, but I could tell he was trying to resist some urge, trying to hold back.

"Please my lord I only wish to serve you, I can offer anything you would like to quell your hunger."

"I doubt very much that you can, I have no taste for servants, please let me return to my solitude."

Taken aback by his words I was unsure of how to continue my approach. But I had not got this far to turn back. Closer I stepped until I was so close that if I stretched out my arm, I could have touched him. I smiled and again offered my services.

"Please my lord, you looked troubled, and I merely want to help soothe your obvious discomfort. What is it your hunger and I will try and appease this appetite of yours?"

I was so close to him, our bodies in contact as I brushed my breasts against him. There was no doubt that he was trying so hard to resist, I could feel his breath from parted lips. His head was turned to the side, and an expression of pure concentration knitted his features.

He wanted me, I could tell that he was on the verge of devouring me and then I felt an arm around my waist and another upon my face tilting it away from him. I could not believe my pure joy as he leaned into me pressing warm lips to my neck, kissing it softly. A delicious feeling as he drew kisses on my skin, so warm, so hungry. Then he kissed so hard it was if he was trying to mark my skin, I cried out slightly as the mixture of pain and pleasure caught me off guard, it was indeed a deep kiss. I felt myself grow weak in his arms how glorious. I wanted him to take me there and then but without warning, he withdrew his lips, and my sweet torture was over.

Still caught in his arms with a strange tingling where he had kissed me; it felt like blood had been drawn, a small warm trail down my neck but I took no notice; instead, I looked up to study his face wondering why he had withdrawn from such a heated embrace. His eyes were no longer focused on me; they looked full of guilt and regret. I followed the gaze, and his arms release me so that I could turn to see the form of Yue-ren standing in the doorway. A picture she was, as beautiful as freshly fallen snow, but her eyes looked as though tears would spill from them any moment.

"So you are just a monster! Well, feed all you like, but my flesh shall not be yours."

It was all she said before she left and I chuckled to myself before pulling myself into Cain. Instead of the embrace, I hoped from him, it was cold and unwelcoming.

"Don't you understand that it wasn't your body I wanted? It wasn't a sexual hunger that drew me to you, it was just hunger. You were nothing more than a snack to feed me, not a very appetising one at that. Now if you excuse me, I have to return to the one I do desire, and I suggest you forget this encounter ever happened unless next time you want me to drain every last drop from your oh so willing body."

And on that note he was gone, not even a glance behind him, just straight to follow Yue-ren. I stood alone biting my bottom lip till I drew blood. The anger welled up in me, how could he treat me like I was nothing? I didn't understand at all. I lifted my hand to my neck and indeed felt a mark, in fact, two small dots and a trail of blood was now drying around them. It was not possible, such things did not exist; I had to shake such irrational thoughts out of my head, besides I had just been rejected which made my desire only more significant. If Cain would not come so easily then it would be even more fun to try and seduce him, I did like a challenge.

My hand went back to the marks on my neck; the thought still lingered, and so did Yue-ren's words. Why did she call Cain a monster? These marks, so much like in stories of…, no, can it be? What am I thinking? And then I heard it, a voice not my own, a voice that sounded seductive and evil at the same time. It rang out from the darkness telling me one thing, a little fact that made Cain more enticing than he had ever been before.

One simple word.

"Vampire."

Chapter 15

Yue-ren

A MOON TO BURN OR DROWN

I couldn't believe it.

I had waited so long, and in the end, the one person that inspired any passion or true emotion was a monster. I walked the halls as fast as I could not believing the sight I had just seen, it was not like he had betrayed me, that maid had been food to him not anything sexual. Something hurt inside me; maybe I had wanted Cain to love me as much as I did him so that the only one he would want to feast upon in any way was me. Was I selfish or was it because nothing in my life had brought me any joy that I had finally decided to give my life to Cain.

My time with Annabel had been the only time I was truly happy outside, but that memory was burnt to ash, too painful to revisit. If I had offered myself to him he could have turned me, they say there is a great pleasure that comes with a vampire's dark kiss, and I had wanted that pleasure to have been mine, not some maids. I made it to my current quarters, and I should have known he would beat me there since he no longer hid his true nature.

"Why did you run? You know what I am. Did you

expect me to starve myself while I waited for you to return to me?"

His words were a mixture of hurt and anger like I had betrayed him in some way! He seemed to grow in size, and his shadow seemed to engulf me.

"You said you had waited long for me, yet you couldn't wait a little longer, you had to go to a maid?"

I began to doubt what I was saying. I kept thinking I was selfish; of course, he would be angry. When he tried to embrace me, I pushed him away, and he is what he is, how could I understand the hunger that must dwell within him. But then he looked at me in anger and spoke again.

"You push me away when you know I burn with passion for you and you alone. I would never force things from you, but I have watched so long from the shadows battling with feelings of love and lust. Yet you still resist what I see in your eyes, but such are my feelings. I still didn't force anything from you, but understand my hunger for you is great and if I cannot indulge in your flesh the only thing I can indulge in is blood. I am a vampire, and my lust for blood is strongest when my emotion is highest. And forbidden passion makes me hungrier than anything."

He paused and I knew he was trying to make me understand his nature and what I was doing to him. And as he talked of lust and passion mine began to grow. He wanted to devour me, such dark need. I had not really understood how the hunger of pleasure would turn into the desire for blood but the fact it had made me crave him. The passion of a vampire; I had longed for love and had got something more, all my life I had hated myself, when there was someone being tortured by the very sight of me. He had begun to walk towards me and I could feel the heat rise inside me. What was I feeling? What was this sensation that shivered through my body, was it lust? Had the very carnal nature of the man before me awakened some new beast within me? His eyes looked at me as they always had but now I realised what he had been holding back, he was prepared to kill for me, to commit murder so that he would not force me into anything. To think that someone would go to such a length for me, to commit a sin such as murder so that he would incur no sin to me.

"The maid was nothing to me, she offered herself, and all I wanted was to drink so that I could tame my feelings for you and you would no longer feel threatened by me."

His words were sincere as he closed the distance between us.

"I want you, all of you, but I will wait as long as you want. But do not push me away as my passion burns with a dangerous intensity and one day I will burn you, you will taste the flames of a vampire's desire."

I was already burning, I felt hot, my face must be burning, but I did not want him to leave. I was no longer afraid, too long I had been ice, and now I was about to melt. His hand was upon my face pulling me into him as I smelt the faint tang of blood on his breath before his lips were against mine. Deep and savage was the kiss, I felt teeth graze the bottom of my lips, but I didn't resist. His other hand held onto my waist gently rubbing his thumb across the bruise there as if to reassure me, to erase the memory from my skin. Slowly he guided me backwards until I felt the bed behind me. Both my hands were gripping the front of his shirt pulling me into him; I wanted him, I needed to feel the closeness as we both tumbled onto the bed, his weight heavy on top of me. The hand that had held my waist had reached lower beneath my dress as I felt strong fingers stroke my leg reaching higher, pressing across my thigh.

The kiss ended; I could feel the bruised lips throbbing from the passionate battle of lips. His mouth began to tease, kissing a trail down my neck and on to my collarbone, leaving marks. He used his other arm to prop himself up so he could look down at me, his blond hair cascaded down each side of his face.

"If this is too much ask me to stop, I promise I will not hurt you for you are my love, my obsession, my desire, you are mine but also I am yours."

I couldn't talk, I tried to form words, but his hand was again trailing a line along my naked thigh. One of my hands held onto the bed sheets, the other was in my mouth so I could muffle the sounds of my yelps. I was ashamed of the sound I had made, no one had touched me like this, and it was evident by the way my body lent into every touch and kiss. His eyes were full of understanding, and a small smile played on his lips as if to say, "Trust me."

Half of me shook with fear, the other half shook with pleasure, but all of me wanted more, wanted him.

Then there was a knock, such bad timing! I could have screamed with frustration. Why now? Why when I had made a decision to stop hiding from my own desires and now that Cain had finished trying to protect me from himself but show me how much his heart and body needed me.

"Miss Yue-ren, an important message for you, the one who left the letter said it was urgent, and you must read it immediately. Please let me in, the messenger was frantic that you read this, I must be let in, please."

I couldn't believe the bad luck; I wanted to shout at her to leave, but the poor girl outside the door sounded upset, a panicked tone in her voice. Cain saw the look in my eyes and released his hold of me.

"I understand; this can wait. Now that I know your resistance is crumbling we can continue this later. Let's see how you deal with pent-up feelings of lust with no release, it shall make our affair even more passionate. Besides I think I shall go for a walk now, it is dark enough to do so, the night air is good for one such as myself."

He had a playful smile, a look I had not seen, almost smug as though he knew he would get exactly what he wanted when he returned and I would be the one suffering as I would have to wait for him with no idea how long he would be. He kissed me gently on the cheek and rose from the bed drawing me up with him. I tried to put myself back in order so as not to appear too dishevelled and opened the door to the young maid. Cain excused himself with not even a glance at the maid, and I watched him walk down the corridor out of sight. I looked at the maid, and my expression changed.

It was the girl from before, her hair tied back so more of her face could be seen and a scarf around her neck to hide the marks Cain had left upon her.

"May I come in my lady? I have something of utmost importance to tell you."

I let her in, feeling sorry that she had been injured because of me and my resistance to Cain. She entered my room, and as I closed the door, I was ready for any questions and accusations she may have for me.

"Well Miss Yue-ren, with that look on your face I guess you realise I have no urgent message, but still I have a message for you."

"Cain will be mine!"

I had to run it through my mind again, not sure what to say as her face twisted in anger.

"You look confused, well let me explain. I know what he is and it doesn't scare me. On the contrary, it rather excites me. You don't deserve a thing of such passion, in fact, I have no idea what he sees in you, you're a weak, pathetic girl made of glass. I will win Cain, to think if I had left it later you would have finally seduced him to your bed but I saved him from that."

Her words were bitter, how could she know?

"I have no idea what you mean. Cain is with me out of choice and believe me, he has no intentions of letting some maid come anywhere near him. He may have fed off you but that means nothing, it was your blood he wanted, not you. So if you could be so kind, please leave and if you value this job don't show yourself in my presence again."

I couldn't believe this girl, how could she really think she had a chance with Cain? I was not about to let anyone steal my happiness. I could feel the atmosphere change in the room, a sense of dread crept up on me. There was nervous energy to this girl, eyes like serpents and hair of rage, she was like a coiled spring. I could sense anger and venom, and it frightened me. It was time for this poisonous snake to go before it bit me. I turned to open the door, but before I could, she cried out,

"You bitch! I will kill you, and then Cain will be mine!"

Out of the corner of my eye, I saw her leap at me, and a flash of light revealed a blade she had kept hidden. The viper had struck, teeth ready for the kill. She was trying to slice at me, but I held her arms as we wrestled for dominance. I wish I had been more masculine for at a time like this I had none of a man's strength and she had me pinned well to the floor. I knocked the blade loose, and it hit the ground with a sharp clang as I used what strength I had to push her off me. Strange what power you can muster when your life is threatened or when you finally realise you have something to fight for.

But as she was pushed back, she grabbed my clothes, ripping my dress to reveal my pale chest. Laughter filled the room then, her high-pitched laughter and it was aimed at me.

"A man! The great beauty and talent Yue-ren is a man! Wait till the world finds out, what a scandal. I thought you were a pathetic woman, but you're an even more pathetic man. No, worse, you're a freak! Does Cain realise how you have deceived him? Does he realise you are just a sick pervert? All this jealousy over such a messed up piece of nothing like you."

Oh, she laughed and laughed, I felt broken, my secret out and no idea what to do. I pulled my clothes together to hide the proof of my deception, but it was too late she had seen, she knew what I was. Her laughter rang in my head. I could feel tears in my eyes and anger growing deep inside me as I edged away from her. Then my fingertips felt it, the cold feeling of metal, a sharp touch and I knew I had found the knife. What was I supposed to do? I couldn't really kill her because she knew my secret, but she would no doubt use the knowledge to ruin me.

Another thought hit me; what of Cain? What would people say if they found out I was in love with another man? I realised I was still a weak person and was not ready to let people find out about me. I wouldn't be able to handle the scorn, the prejudice and the hatred. I couldn't let everything go to ruin, I was finally happy. This place was not like the world I had lived in with Annabel and her family, a world that judged you on the strength of your character and the deeds you committed. For a moment that cold feeling returned.

I had nearly forgotten all about that life and what it had taught me, to respect myself and that I would be loved for the person I am regardless of my gender. That time spent in a loving family had made me ready for a new life and while it had been cruelly snatched from me, forgetting what I had learnt from them would be a sin.

If they knew I was dwelling in perceived weakness,

Annabel would have called me on it. I have lost a family but not what I learnt from them. For the first time, it was not tears of shame and self-pity that threatened to spill from my eyes, I cried for the family I lost but also the guilt that I had not brought honour to their memory. I felt fresh tears of joy knowing that I wanted to live and pursue my own happiness and my own life.

"What are you going to do you freak, kill me? My, my, a grown man crying, it's sick. Why don't you give me the knife and I can put you out of your misery? I can make it, so no one ever knew your secret, even in death, then you will be free and so will Cain. Now come let me end it."

She came towards me her hand grasped my wrist, the blade trembling in my hand. What do I do? I felt her push it towards me changing the angle so it would strike me in the chest and in a second, things were no longer clear. I panicked. I tried to throw it away, that's what I meant to do, but at the same time I did she lunged forward. In the end, I was stronger it seemed, as the blade was impaled into her chest. Crimson blood began to spill out on to my hands, clothes and feet as she stumbled back from me.

"What have you done? Not only are you sick, but you're also a freak and now a murderer."

It was all she could say pulling the blade from her and letting it fall to the floor. Blood stained her clothes, it was everywhere as she dropped to her knees then forwards into the growing puddle before her. I could only watch as the puddle grew larger and began to run towards my feet. What had I done? I had taken a human life, I had significantly sinned, and I was helpless. In blind panic I fled; I ran out of my room, down halls, into the night. I did not care about the pool of blood nor the trail I was probably leaving. I did not care that a striking white figure dipped in red black blood would probably stand out if seen. For once I hoped my ghost-like appearance meant I would not be chased or stopped. No, all I could hear was my heart thumping and the rhythm of my feet upon the ground as wood turned to stone.

I had to find Cain, I had to.

I had no one else to turn to, nothing to go back to.

Chapter 16

Yue-ren

THE HAUNTING OF THE MOON

THE NIGHT WAS THICK AND HEAVY SPILLING FORTH ITS darkness into the cold room.

The figure lay beneath blankets, body exhausted from spent emotion. Yue-ren had still not managed to move from the bed, his head resting on tear damped pillows. His eyes were red, stained by the tears he had shed and his voice was weak as he tried to call out into the darkness. He could not completely remember how he had arrived in this dark room with its blocked windows. It was not an unfriendly room; it had ornate wooden furnishing, deep red walls with blood red drapes and he lay upon a luxurious bed. From the bed he could smell Cain's scent, thick and heavy and powerful, maybe that's why he felt less comfortable here, he wasn't used to being in a place that was so devoid of life and yet felt oppressive and overpowering.

And how did he come to be lying in Cain's bed?

He had to think back, but that was the last thing he wanted to do for the memory of what had just occurred was too strong. He was now a murderer, he had killed that young woman, and why? Because he was afraid, his secret would be revealed. He was distraught, his clothes torn and covered with her blood as he ran from his home that night; he had run out into the cold dark world with no thought as to where he was going. The night air chilled him, his eyes stung from tears and his feet were caked in the dirt of the streets, no one would recognise the opera star Yue-ren looking like this. He knew the news of the murder would soon sweep through this town; the scandal of Yue-ren being male would be overshadowed by Yue-ren the murderer. So Yue-ren slunk into the shadows, down the dirty and uninhabited passageways where no one treads. It was here he sank to the floor amongst the unseen filth of a perfect city; a city that's extreme beauty blinded people to whatever dirt could lurk beneath its skin, it is here that Yue-ren felt he belonged.

Yue-ren did not remember much after that, strong arms had lifted him, and a familiar scent came from the body he was now cradled against. He remembered eyes of gold staring into him as if they were trying to rip through him, burn out the details as to how Yue-ren had ended up in such a condition.

All Yue-ren could say was one word: 'Lillian'.

A mixture of warmth and anger could be felt from the being that was carrying him. It wasn't until he felt clean and comfortable did he realise he was in Cain's bed, for who else's would have this familiar scent and who else's eyes would look upon him so fiercely? But Cain was nowhere to be seen at the moment, and Yue-ren had no idea where he might be. Again Cain had saved him, again he had found him, cradled him and protected him and for the first time, Yue-ren wasn't grateful. So much had happened to him; he had seen and been through so much, and yet he still felt weak and fragile. He was tired of being rescued, he and Cain had finally met; wasn't he saved already? Wasn't it time for him to start feeling alive and safe? No, he didn't want safety and protection; he wanted to feel love but more than that, passion.

He had shed tears, and he had felt pathetic all his life, but now there was something more. He had seen so much death and knew suffering, sadness, loneliness and depression, and now all he wanted was for the fire of Cain's passion to burn all these emotions out of him until he was nothing but a body that burned with need and desire.

He had killed, that he couldn't take back, but his life was his own. He couldn't return to the opera, its final memory too painful for him to live with. He would make a new life, a free life, start again and this time let no useless tears and unwanted emotions take hold of his body. Laughter had begun to fill the room, a smile playing on Yue-ren's lips. Had he suffered so much, had his body gone through so much pain that now his mind was beginning to suffer? Wasn't there a young girl's blood on his hands? Shouldn't he feel guilt now life was snatched away because of his selfishness? But then again hadn't she been trying to take the one thing that brought him joy?

Lillian had wanted Cain and that Yue-ren couldn't allow. Cain was Yue-ren's saviour; he was going to take away all those sad and painful memories and carve a new life, mark his body with desire and passion so that no other emotion and sensation would mean anything. Yes, that night Yue-ren thought he wanted passion, he didn't want tears, so sick of worrying about others and their lives, all that mattered was his life. A life with Cain, a man so full of passion, lust and power that Yue-ren would feel things he only ever dreamed of before. Having a vampire for a lover meant he'd never fear anything again if any creature would know how to make one's blood stir it would be a vampire, a creature of carnal passion, a man to devour you, mind, spirit and flesh. Hadn't he been about to give himself entirely to Cain?

He lifted his hands to his lips. That kiss had been demanding and possessive; it had fuelled him and made him feel alive and desperate to be possessed.

"My, my, what's so funny? You don't at all look like someone who's just killed a person".

Yue-ren turned to see a young woman dressed in a traditional red dress that cascaded off her to the floor and sat just off her shoulders revealing a slender neck. Red hair fell about her face, full and vibrant much like her deep red lips that were curled into a cruel smile.

"Lillian, I thought, I thought…"

Yue-ren's voice was weak and came as a whisper as he confronted the vision before him staring fearfully and whispering, "It can't be" to himself.

"Well as you see, it can be, I have been given new life. You see as I lay on the floor, the life flowing out of me, I was given an offer I couldn't refuse. I thank being here to my new father. He has renamed me Lillith, so please be as kind to address me by that name. Now don't look so shocked, my new father is a powerful and generous being, it only cost me my soul to get my body back. Of course I'm not really alive either, but I'm also not dead. In fact, I've never been more like Cain, as I too am immortal now. Don't worry, I'm not here to kill you either, my revenge will be far slower. I just wanted to make sure you're not trying to forget me or what you did to me. Oh and also that I haven't given up on Cain, I will make him mine."

Lillith sounded so confident and calm as if everything that had occurred was natural. She stood there staring, no malice showing on her face or in her eyes, instead smiling. Yue-ren couldn't move. He felt shocked and confusion; had all the tragedy in his life finally made him snap? Was this a vision or hallucination? And just like that, in the blink of an eye, she was gone as if she had never been there as time slowed and Yue-ren was left standing with only silence and darkness to answer him. Who knew how long Yue-ren stood there staring into the empty space Lillith had occupied. Time had lost meaning until the atmosphere in the room changed. A hand was placed on his shoulder, and immediately his skin felt warm. Passionate breath on the back of his neck as a low voice spoke to him.

"What happened at the opera? There was a great pool of blood, so much that whoever had been hurt is surely dead. Before you fear, all signs of death and blood have been cleared away as if nothing happened but I would have you tell me what occurred."

Cain was calm as the hand on Yue-ren's shoulder tightened, and he stepped forward until Yue-ren's back was pressed against Cain, Cain pulled him even closer with an arm wrapped possessively round Yue-ren's waist.

"I killed her. She came to challenge me, she came to take you away from me. We argued, and she threatened me, she wanted me dead, she wanted me ruined. She found out what I really am and I was weak. I killed her; I saw the knife go in, I felt it cut, I felt the warm blood flow onto me. She should be dead."

Yue-ren was trembling; he wanted to be strong, he wanted to be confident as he turned in Cain's arms to face him, eyes challenging Cain.

"Make it go away, make everything go away! I want to forget that opera house. I want to forget myself. I want you to give me new memories, new life, a new passion. I won't let a spectre scare me. I won't give you up to the phantoms of my mind. I want you to erase everything about this world until the only things that are left are our bodies and our desires."

Cain lent down to kiss Yue-ren, the distance closing between them until out of the corner of his eye Yue-ren saw her standing there behind Cain looking calm and confident again.

"Why are you here? Let me be! I don't care about you, Cain is mine!"

"Yue-ren, there's no one there, who are you screaming at? I will not play games with you, don't tease or test me now."

"She's there watching us; a ghost, a phantom, I don't know what but I will not have her haunt me. Aren't you a vampire? Have you not age, experience and great power? Why can't you sense her? Why do you not chase her away?"

Yue-ren felt great anger as he screamed. Why wasn't Cain trying to get rid of her? Cain held his ground, patience wearing thin; he could see no spectre, feel no ghostly presence.

"Come to your senses Yue-ren, madness is trying to grasp at you. What do you know of vampires? Yes I am old and powerful, I have lived long enough to see new magic turn into old technology but I can't do magic, I can't chase away imaginary foes. We have come too far to let the ghost of a girl stop us; be strong, how many people do you think I have killed? Do you think I let them haunt me? Remember I am not here to save you or protect you. I am a dark creature, and I swear to posses you, to spend an eternity making your every desire come true, to show you pleasure until your body cannot survive unless I am feasting on it. Have you forgotten that moment in your room when you were to give yourself to me? This is your desire as much as mine."

Cain's grip was tight, his words echoing and dangerous as Yue-ren pulled away trying to back away from the spectre staring at him. But again Lillith disappeared, and

Yue-ren could only look about in panic until he heard words being whispered in his ear.

"I am always watching you, this is my revenge to watch you go mad until Cain himself can no longer stomach your insecurity. You will never be alone again dear boy."

And with that, she was gone, and Yue-ren could only do one thing. His scream echoed all through the room, high and shrill, he screamed until his throat was raw until he hardly had breath in him and then the world went dark on him. Cain saw him sway and caught him before he could hit the floor. Cain placed Yue-ren in his bed, again denied when so close and left angry and full of desire with no outlet. He needed to go out, he needed to hunt.

He couldn't just stay and look on the slender frame of the one he desired, knowing he had the strength to force him but promised he wouldn't.

Chapter 17

Cain

THE SUN GROWS WEARY

Cain knew something was wrong, he could sense it with every fibre of his being.

The scent of desperation and fear was in the air, and he could feel it, he could sense that great pain and suffering had been caused this night and at once he knew something had happened to his beloved. The night air sang of tragic events and tasted of the tears that had been shed into it. No other creature would have been able to sense and taste all the emotions that were swirling in the breeze of the night, but Cain knew that he had to find Yue-ren.

He followed the feeling of dread and fear moving like a shadow across the rooftops of the city. Each roof a maze of spires, hidden passages, slanted ledges and snarling creatures standing in their perpetual stone prisons. He knew these rooftops like the back of his hand; he could navigate them without looking and often sought the comfort of their dark shadows and hidden dwellings. But tonight he tore past the stone creatures that inhabited them, didn't even take a second look at their fine spires or rest in the dark shadows these spires cast. No, he had somewhere to be, Yue-ren was waiting somewhere in this city, alone and frightened. He knew that Yue-ren would have gone somewhere to hide, somewhere void of people to see him and while they were a perfect place for Cain to hide, a normal human would never be able to climb them or negotiate them. But the rooftops weren't the only place in this city for a person to disappear to; no, like all cities there were those places unseen by many and forgotten by most.

This was not because these places were invisible; it was because most people ignored them and pretended they didn't exist. The lonely corridors that separated the great buildings of this city, the walkways devoid of all life and filled with things that everyone would most like to forget.

No city is without its filth, and these dark passageways were where it was put, so the aristocrats didn't have to look at their own waste. Early in the morning before decent society would wake, silent machines would travel down these pathways taking away the refuse and filth. They worked quickly and in secret and once they had picked up all they could they would disappear with their load.

No one knew how they got in or out of the city without notice; in fact, many didn't even know of their existence, it was one of those never spoken about matters. After all, what aristocrat would be brave enough to ask another where their waste and unmentionables went? Cain may be the only person to have ever seen them, the silent workers of metal and even then he only saw them in winter when it remained darker a little longer. They would come up through manholes he imagined, gleaming as they caught the morning sun in the summer and go about their task. Small metal claws picking up every form of rubbish they could find never questioning what they picked up. Each would carry its fill until it could lift no more and then it would descend back down the manhole leaving no trace of its existence.

And now to think the one he loved and desired more than anything was sitting among the unmentionable trash of the city tainting his very being with the filth that people were too afraid to even admit they made. It was a horrible thought, one as beautiful as Yue-ren should never be seen sitting in waste, should never have to know about how dirty people can be. It was then Cain caught the smell of blood in the air, blood he recognised. It wasn't fair like Yue-ren's, this odour was that of the maid from the opera. That cruel and vulgar girl, why was it her scent he could smell? He followed it down into the dark corridors; it was awful the smell of this place and so many different smells of blood. Old blood, new blood, tainted blood, rotting blood, pure blood and blood of innocence. But amongst the smells, he could also sense a human presence crying into the darkness, a lost soul, a soul losing its direction.

He was glad for his night eyesight for there he saw his beloved, his Yue-ren sitting amongst rubbish on the floor. Yue-ren's clothes and hair were caked in muck, and he smelt of blood. What had happened to him? His beautiful light, a creature of grace, elegance and innocence, now looking like the corpse of a victim Cain had devoured in a bloody rage?

He got closer and was shocked to see Yue-ren's clothes torn and his arms bruised. He lifted up his treasure and smelt that cruel girl's scent, had she been the one to do this to his beautiful boy? She would pay for this, if she wanted a vampire this much, she would have one. Cain would find her and rip out her heart, he would tear into her jugular and drink her dry. She would look in horror as she was treated worse than food, he wouldn't savour her flavour he would show no appreciation for the taste and warmth of her blood.

He would merely drain her and discarded her as a mere treat to stave off hunger or entertain him a little while before he found something better to play with. But before he could satisfy his thirst for bloodshed and vengeance, he had to take Yue-ren somewhere safe, somewhere he could be clean and comfortable. Yue-ren had to be returned to the vision of beauty he once was. Cain would bring him warmth and kiss away every pain. He would make Yue-ren feel like he did earlier that day, passionate and hungry.

He lifted Yue-ren into the night; they soared into the darkness and across Cain's maze of rooftops until they stood on the balcony of a luxurious mansion. Through the open balcony door, Cain strode entering a large room that held nothing but a grand piano and its seat. The room had no windows bar the large doorway he had walked through, there were no pictures or mirrors on the walls of the room, no lighting could be seen, not even candlesticks. The room was pitch black; no human could have been able to see much in here even with the moonlight shining in to reveal the piano.

As Cain walked across the room to the window, the doorway closed behind him, and thick red drapes closed about it. They were now in complete darkness as Cain strode through the room until another door opened in front of him leading to a dark corridor. Cain had never thought to install lights to his home, what use was lighting for someone who could see in the dark? Some of the rooms had, but these were mostly rooms he entertained his dinner guests in and they never really had the time or a chance to see the rest of Cain's home. He, at last, found the door that led to his destination and it opened to reveal a spacious bathroom. Yue-ren was placed in a large, and Cain saw that there were indeed candlesticks in this room.

One of his last guests had said she had wanted to

freshen up for him and had taken the candle into the bath-room with her before her unfortunate departure. Cain did not feel guilt for the fates of these people now that he was about to bath Yue-ren in a room that he had killed and feasted in. What was the point of feeling guilt over those he had killed in the years of Yue-ren's departure? He didn't think the smell of blood would offend Yue-ren. He was human, so the scent of blood that tainted many of these rooms would be too faint for him to pick up on.

Cain removed the torn and dirtied clothes from Yue-ren, discarding them into a rubbish shoot that would lead to one of those passageways waiting to be whisked away by the city's small metal workers. Fresh warm water filled the bath, but Cain didn't plug it instead he let the water drain, taking away the filth and blood from Yue-ren's body.

Brown water washed away revealing that fair milky skin of alabaster. Yue-ren's body was slightly warmer to touch and felt smooth under Cain's strong hands. Cain continued to wash away the dirt from his beloved's body, careful to use soaps that wouldn't be too harsh. He gently removed the soil from Yue-ren's hair, delicately stroking his fingers through the white tresses. He worked slowly making sure he was thorough and took his time to watch Yue-ren's skin react to the warm water and gentle ministra-tion of his hands. He couldn't help but smile as he slid his hand over Yue-ren's skin to wipe away both dirt and soap. After all, he should be allowed this guilty pleasure of looking at this beautiful boy's naked and wet form. His desire for revenge soon changed and how he wished Yue-ren would wake up and surrender to him so he could have his way with him there and then.

But there was no pleasure in taking a sleeping person, he wanted Yue-ren awake and wanting. After he was cleaned Cain draped him in towels and carried him away from the bathroom.

They soon entered another room, again dark and painted in deep reds and filled with drapes and tapestries, many hiding boarded up windows. Cain removed the towels and placed Yue-ren into one of his shirts before lowering him into his bed. His bed, he thought to himself, at last Yue-ren was in his bed but still not able to receive the pleasure Cain wanted to rain down on him.

Cain placed a kiss on Yue-ren's lips; he knew that when he awoke, he would be disorientated but he would soon realise he was in Cain's bed. Even without Cain's presence, the room was still filled with his aura. Cain left his treasure to sleep as he went to find out what happened at the opera. Tonight he would see some desire fulfilled. He would have his vengeance, he would taste blood, and he would go home and have Yue-ren's sweet surrender to him.

Through the night he moved like smoke in the wind, like rainwater to the river, like fire in the forest and soon he was standing outside the opera house. It looked old and unfeeling, a depressed building that had seen horror and was now fed up and exhausted. It didn't seem or feel grand, it was dark and empty. Its visitors had long since departed to sleep off their full night of joyous indulgence, and the maids and servants had gone to sleep after their work had been done.

He drifted through passageways and doors like smoke until he was standing in Yue-ren's room. Yue-ren's scent was strong in here, but he could tell that the room's last memory of Yue-ren was not a beautiful one. The air was thick with death and fear, and there on the ground was a large puddle of blood. Cain knew it wasn't from his treasure, there had been no wounds on Yue-ren's body, and from the smell, he could tell it was the maid girl's blood.

What had happened here? Had she come to challenge Yue-ren? Yue-ren's clothes had been torn, they must have fought. She would have torn Yue-ren's dress to reveal a pale chest, the chest of a man; she would have threatened to ruin him. If Cain had been there he would have struck her down where she stood, he would never have allowed her to lay a hand on what was his, let alone threaten him. Yue-ren couldn't have killed her, he was a gentle and innocent soul, but she had definitely been wounded.

Cain tried to see a body, but there was none. Did the girl survive? Had she gone to find help? If so why wasn't there blood anywhere else? Surely there would have been a trail? Was she found? But then why hadn't anyone called the police or an ambulance? There was no sign of them; the area hadn't been cordoned off, no police were guarding the door or the opera at all, and there certainly wasn't anyone about the city looking for Yue-ren as surely he would have been a suspect?

Cain could not understand it, but he had to make sure no matter where the girl's body was that no evidence could point back to his Yue-ren, for a lot of blood could be seen on the floor and losing that much blood would inevitably lead to death. Cain stepped up to the pool of blood and almost immediately it began to run from him. It was as if the blood itself was scared of Cain even though a vampire would never drink spilt blood it still feared being that close.

Every single drop of the dark sticky liquid ran, trickling and collecting together until it had nowhere to go. The pool of blood collected against a wall swirling into a ball of viscous red liquid. Once every drop had joined this ball, Cain held out his hand, and the swirling mass of blood floated into it. He stood there as this mass of blood twirled in his hand dancing like the current of the river but with nowhere to flow. He slowly closed his hand. The swirling mass became smaller and smaller until all that was left was a little dark pellet lying in the palm of his hand.

He stared at it; the pellet resembled a red pebble, the deepest red with a shiny surface. It could have passed as an exquisite jewel, and only Cain would know that it was a bloodstone. He slipped the stone into his pocket as he had a place to store these fine bloodstones at home and turned to the rest of the room. Nothing looked out of place; without the blood, you would hardly know a struggle had gone on. Pieces of ripped clothes could be seen, but Cain quickly disposed of them, sending them spiralling down the nearby rubbish chute. The room looked normal and free of incriminating evidence and yet something was odd.

Cain could feel something else had been here, no human, he would have smelt human. No, this was the fragrance of something far less common. Whatever it was he didn't feel like investigating it, not while the form of Yue-ren could be awake and waiting for him in his bed.

If the girl was already dead, then there was no need for vengeance, and if by some fluke she was alive then he would soon find her. But now it was more important to comfort his beautiful boy. Cain left the opera; he would probably not need to return here. He would take Yue-ren away from this city; he would take him to a wondrous new place. There were many of these extravagant cities all over this world, why confine themselves to one? He would show Yue-ren all the wonders of the world, but first, he wanted to show him all the pleasure of the flesh. He had done so much travelling this night he was glad to finally step back into his own home. He hoped it was for the last time as he was well aware of the time and didn't want to risk not being able to return till the next night.

What occurred next had not been what Cain had expected at all. Yue-ren had been stood in the room, and

Cain had gone to get some kind of explanation from him. Instead, Yue-ren had seemed wild and angry and pleaded with Cain to make it all go away. Who was Cain to deny his love what he wanted and as he bent down to kiss and comfort and claim his love Yue-ren snapped again.

The whole conversation, if it could be called that, had seemed ridiculous. Cain could sense no ghost, no phantom, there was nothing but the two of them and Cain was tired of waiting for Yue-ren, and now he was being denied again. Things were becoming more and more frustrating. Yue-ren had asked for desire and now was screaming at some unseen enemy. What made it worse was Yue-ren's assumptions that he could just chase away a fictitious foe. He was tired of teasing, he was tired of being this protector and saviour, and he was a creature of the night not the champion of an insecure boy.

He wanted them to indulge in desires and passions. He had tried to make Yue-ren come to his senses but knew that his anger was apparent and his grip had become tight and forceful. Were they never to get peace? Where no one's wishes ever to be answered? He had given Yue-ren time and space. He had quelled his own nature for this fair creature and what had it gotten him? Was someone playing a cruel joke on them? Was someone trying to get between them? Was something else made of dark power also after Yue-ren's innocence and beauty? Did someone else have a claim on the one thing Cain truly desired, the one creature he could love?

But before the thought could go much further, Yue-ren began to scream a haunting and terrified scream. It was like something was crawling its way through his mind trying to tear out all his emotions. It was as if any moment blood would spill from those lips and Yue-ren's throat would tear open with all the anguish that was being concealed in his troubled mind.

Then he stopped, eyes glassed over as he began to fall to the floor and was caught in Cain's arms. Cain placed him in the bed, covered him in sheets and then left the room. To the night he would take as he had much frustration to work out and only a few hours of nightfall to indulge in. He was sick of fate's cruel game, and again the thoughts of someone playing with him and Yue-ren came to his mind. Somewhere out there someone could be challenging him to his claim.

Maybe, just maybe, something else was out there.

Chapter 18

Laphiel

THE FULL GREED OF THE STORM

LAPHIEL SMIRKED TO HIMSELF.

What fun he was having watching all the players put on such an entertaining show. Cain with his confidence trying not to admit that he had fallen in love and was now acting on the human emotions he always denied as a so-called 'creature of the night'. The vampire was still in denial thinking he could have his prize and be allowed to love something that wasn't even his. Beautiful Yue-ren, so much like his mother, beautiful and graceful and yet so lost, going mad from the very fact that he is alive. Lillith, his new and beautiful creation, so much spite and wickedness was in her, a genuinely selfish human girl, well maybe no longer human. Poor girl. If she knew what she really was would she still thank Laphiel for the wonderful gift of giving her new life? Laphiel decided that the games were coming to an end. He already knew that vampire, that poor tamed creature of the night, was on his way back to the opera house and maybe it was time to let that creature know that Yue-ren could never be his.

Laphiel thought back; he remembered all those times

lying with Selina-ren and what a selfish, self-absorbed beauty she was. But she was still too human, full of confidence and superiority. She may have been a beauty to behold, but that was only on the outside. Laphiel wanted someone that had great beauty inside and out. Someone so void of human emotions that they would live for him. Someone that couldn't hate or get angry, someone that could not love so could not feel jealousy or regret. Yue-ren would be that perfect vessel, unable to get close to anyone, unable to live for anyone. It was going to be so easy. Laphiel would come to him, destroy everyone and everything he could possibly care for until it was just the two of them and all Yue-ren had left was Laphiel. An empty beautiful soul just for him to do with as he pleased. Anything Laphiel would have said would have been scripture to this poor lost soul.

He knew that his beauty's mind was fading. Lillith was making sure he could no longer tell reality from imagination which aided his master plan. Yue-ren would have no choice but to live in Laphiel's dream, there was no real world for him. Laphiel was overjoyed; a fantasy world where there was nothing but the most beautiful doll that only lived for him to play with. And if Laphiel got bored of his endless pleasure he would use his powers to feed someone else's soul to Yue-ren. When his beautiful doll thought he may have some kind of life again, there would be Laphiel to help destroy it and rescue his prize back to an endless fantasy. What a beautiful, infinite circle and what made it all so much better was that no one, not even a tamed vampire, could break the connection between Laphiel and Yue-ren. They were a part of each other, a bond of blood and everyone knows that you can't break bonds of blood. The vampire may not have tasted his love's blood, but that was because of what he feared. That if he tastes the blood of his beautiful and pure love he would taste something evil, something dirty and tainted.

There was a demon in Yue-ren, unholy and cursed and proof that he was for Laphiel alone and that vampire could not boast such claims. He then thought back to that poor child he had created, silly foolish girl. She thought she was a demon now. She thought she had great power and was using it to achieve her goals. It was Laphiel that was masking her presence from Cain. After all, her soul was now his. She had sold her soul; her body was nothing more than decaying flesh being held together by Laphiel's will. Once he was bored, she would just crumble and fade. Her soul was worth very little, so impure and disgusting, filled with vile thoughts and polluted ambitions. Maybe he would feed it to Yue-ren one day and watch as he felt dirty and unclean. That could be a fun game; Yue-ren disgusted by what he thought were his thoughts and desires and Laphiel there for him to act out those horrible desires. His own disgust would drive him mad, and eventually, he would have to have his soul from him, and he would have to concede to the life of a soulless doll again. What a fun idea indeed and the only thing in the way was a stupid vampire that can't make up his mind what his true nature is.

The vampire was close. He could sense bloodlust and anger in the air. Ah yes, this creature of the night was in a rage and out for blood. But there was only a little time before dawn, what exactly did he think he was going to accomplish in such a short space of time? Would he be able to just stay in the opera house and leave his poor love aban-doned to be tortured by a foe he couldn't see? Foolish vampire. Sometimes they really do let their nature take over, so angry and ready to kill that they lose common sense. So much a human trait for a creature that swears it's beyond humanity. He wondered if Cain had let the irony of this sink in. Laphiel thought to himself that as a demon he had no such emotion. Everything was just a game, something to play and as long as he was happy others didn't matter. He got what he wanted, and no creature should be stupid enough to try and tell him otherwise.

Laphiel sat in a grand room where Selina-ren would entertain her wealthiest and luxurious guests. The sofas were a beautiful mahogany brown colour and made of expensive leather. He was draped across the very seat the great Selina-ren would have resided in. The ceiling was a little lower compared to the great halls and guest rooms, but that was to make for a more intimate atmosphere. An atmosphere that would be heavy with drink, smoke and desire. A row of candles lit the room, each made of cast iron and in the shape of a slender vine branching into three roses for the candles to sit in. So typical of women with more money than sense, who believed themselves to be gothic aristocrats. The room had no windows, it was a room designed for the most personal of guests. Anything that happened in here was never to escape not even through the tiniest of gaps in a sealed window. The carpet was thick and the colour of burgundy. How it kept so clean was always a mystery. After a decadent night in Selina-ren's special guest room maids were given strict instruction to ask no questions about the room. A professional cleaner would be hired at great expense and then leave again only ever to return when the great room needed cleaning.

Since the passing of Selina-ren, the room had never been used, and the regular maids came in to dust it, never knowing of all the things that had happened in this dark sanctuary of desires and debauchery. It seemed a fitting place for Laphiel to sit and wait for the angry guest he was expecting to arrive. Laphiel had lit the candles and also lit some incense burners to recapture some of the smell this room had been full of in the past. It had been in this very room so long ago when he and the lust-filled Selina-ren had given into sexual desire, and he had ravished her on the floor. If you called it a beautiful act such as making love you would have been very much mistaken. It had been just the two of them, a private party and such a dirty and impure night. No grace or dignity, only two debauched beings indulging in the pleasure of flesh in a room so filled with indulgent passions. It was here that Laphiel had seen the line between something beautiful and something vulgar. It was here where he saw how ugly something beautiful could be and it was this night so long ago that he began to think about creating something he could change at will between his desire for beauty and his passion for filth.

Even though he laid with her many times in many different guises, he knew that she was going to mother his disgustingly beautiful child. He wanted to taste her as much as possible until he felt he had tainted her body enough so it could bear what he wanted. A creature that was his that could be the most beautiful thing to behold and yet be dirty and tainted. Someone he could choose when they rotted and when they bloomed.

"It is time."

Laphiel whispered into the night. The vampire was in the opera house. This was the end of the beginning.

Chapter 19

Cain

THE SCORNFUL HEAT OF THE SUN

The night air felt charged as if swarms of tiny insects were buzzing with anticipation.

It was only a couple of hours till dawn, and the world would come alive again, but for now, the world was quiet apart from the strange sensation in the air. Cain's flesh felt alive as he sped through the night. What was he looking for? Where would he begin his search? He had little time to find a victim to seduce and feed off to quell the feelings inside. He also knew that there was a specific creature out there that was in some way responsible to what was plaguing Yue-ren. So on edge, so on fire; he wanted to claw with frustration at his own skin, like a beast beset with a rash, to get some satisfaction.

He was angry and frustrated.

He wanted blood.

He wanted to see the rich crimson blood stain the floor beneath him and he wanted to rip out the throat of some unfortunate soul and sink his teeth into flesh like a primal beast. Cain had needs, and they weren't being satisfied, and now he could feel all his needs and lust burning just beneath the surface of his skin.

But as much as he wanted to indulge in bloodshed and carnage to relieve his tension he also had another pressing matter to attend to. The Demon, that creature that had claimed that Yue-ren was somehow a part of him and that Cain had no claim on the beautiful boy. Cain knew he must be in this town, somewhere nearby, watching his precious creation go mad. If there really was something tormenting his beloved, then the demon must be behind it, masking its presence from Cain. Foul stinking creature. Cain knew what he had implied, and he didn't want to think about it, he didn't want to think of two so wholly different beings sharing the same blood.

But the possibility was there, otherwise, that Demon would not have told Cain to taste Yue-ren's blood if he could not back up his claims.

No, somewhere in this city the disgusting beast was sitting smiling to himself about how well he had messed up these lives and how he was out doing a vampire at his own game stating he had a claim on a prize a vampire had marked as his.

Cain felt as if his blood would boil; so much anger and frustration burning him to the core, threatening to rip through his flesh like lava. If he was this foul demon where would he hide? Where would he sit and smirk to himself? There was really only one place; the same place Cain himself had stalked waiting for his fair and troubled love to appear. The Opera House. That magnificent building, a beautiful and powerful reconstruction of the ones that had existed in this world hundreds of years ago.

This indulgent world that could create whatever it wanted to please its high-class society.

The Opera house was one of the most beautiful buildings in this reconstructed city. This beautiful city and its gothic buildings with high ceilings and cast iron fences. The people so far into their fantasies they paid no attention to what made their city run, to the power supplies underground and the fact that everything was run on circuits formed of the most evolved technologies. So many mysteries of the world had been discovered, so much science and technology evolved to perfection that now generations later could live off the money their inventor fathers earned without ever stopping to consider how genuinely inspirational and pioneering these past generations were.

These were indulgent times which, to creatures of the night such as himself and that loathsome demon, meant so many more opportunities. Humanity's vanity and self-indulgence had lead to a rise in the mythic creatures of the past; vampires once hunted and feared lived in a time where people couldn't care less about the safety of each other. These aristocratic worlds were a perfect haven as humans lived lives nearly as decadent and debauched of their vampire predators.

Cain had grown fond of this world and what it had allowed him but now things were different; now he had something else in this world he cared for. Cain sailed through the night, his dark form moving at speed no human could detect with compelling grace and elegance. Even jumping from building to building was a majestic dance to a vampire that had lived a full life. But an entire life alone seemed so less fulfilling than the life he wished to share with Yue-ren. As loathe as he was to admit it, even after all this time some small shred of humanity was left. A shred that made him unlike that demon, a shred that meant he wanted to protect Yue-ren and not torture him.

Cain was in love with this fragile human, he knew it

more and more each day, he loved him with a vampire's passion and lust. Such love could destroy a human, particularly one as frail as Yue-ren, but Cain was sick of quelling these feelings. Tonight he would find the demon with his claim and kill him. He would then satisfy his need for blood, and when his need for carnage and death was over, he would return to Yue-ren and satisfy his lust. He knew Yue-ren wanted the same; he wanted a world to be himself far from this fake reconstructed fantasy. He wanted to indulge, feel passion and lust.

He was sick of being broken; within him was the capability to change his wretched life. Cain knew if he released Yue-ren from his bonds he could live with passion knowing he is loved and lusted over by an immortal being. Yue-ren would get stronger and more determined. He and Cain could share a life of pure passion, lust and love indulging in their dreams, coming and going as they like, watching the world and humanity corrupt and fool itself while their simple desire for each other sustained them.

That thought drove the vampire on with even more determination.

He had someone to love and protect but also to indulge in and no demon, no matter his claim, could stand in his way. He landed at the front of the opera house its large haunting door looking down on him judging him as if he was trying to enter the cathedral of Notre Dame. The doors screamed at him, knowing he was full of lust and anger; they didn't want something like that to pollute their private domains. But this was no holy building, no god resided in here. It wasn't a sanctuary for the innocent; it was, in fact, the complete opposite. Breathing deeply, eyes shining brightly as if on fire, Cain walked up the steps. He was too overcome with emotion to try and delicately slip into this building.

He wanted to make his presence known, he wanted his arrival known. His teeth ached with the need for blood; his fingernails as sharp as claws begging to rip through flesh as he placed both hands on the doors. If doors could scream what a cry would have pierced this night as Cain used his strength to open the bolted doors. They creaked and cracked as he forced his way in. The bar that held them shut on the inside made a horrific snapping sound as it snapped in two echoing into the quiet building. The metal ripped, and the façade of a traditional door revealed itself as the metal structure within torn apart, wires sparked, and the hum of electricity could be heard.

For a brief moment Cain thought about who might discover this torn entrance way and would they be shocked to learn it was made of metal and wire or would they even know it had been powered by technology or what that also meant. Ignorant humans, how fast they forget their own creations when their own desires and comforts rule their thinking.

The doors spread themselves, fractured and torn, the bolts and screws that held it in place destroyed like the great bar that had fallen to the floor. Truly damaged, it would take time to fix and heal this wound to the opera house, but Cain did not care. To add to the great noise of his entrance, Cain paused for a moment then drew in his breath before letting a feral scream escape his lungs and pierce through the corridors. He began to hear shuffling and murmurs as the guests and house workers woke. He could hear some murmur in fear asking for someone to go see what wild beast had broken into the opera house.

Little lights could be seen as some rooms lit, but still, no one came to great Cain. He could smell fear in the air, rich and heavy, and once again he breathed deep.

"LAPHIEL!!!" He screamed into the night.

"Where are you foul demon? Show yourself to me, depraved filth!"

He paused to listen to doors creak open but still no one approached.

"Someone show themselves otherwise I'll enter every room till I find that demon!"

He knew what would happen next. Even if these aristocrats were poor excuses of humans compared to the generations that had existed before, he knew that it was human nature to act in a primal manner when scared.

He heard footsteps, a group had gathered, and from the heavy fall of their feet, he knew them to be all male. A light from further down a hall was getting brighter, faux torches had been lit. How ironic. Cain remembered centuries ago when villagers would light torches, pick up pitchforks and form an angry mob to go 'hunt down the monster'. Even later in the old movies, it had been a ridiculous thing to see a bunch of humans and their farm equipment group together to go slay a vampire. But so many years later and here they were again, an angry mob with their weapons ready to chase out the beast. Cain did not want to play this game, it was old and time was short if he wanted to return to Yue-ren this night.

He walked up the corridor to meet the increasingly loud group who had now started to shout at him. The same old clichéd lines but unlike the villagers of old that were hardened and strengthened by working in fields or before the luxuries of science and technology, this group was made up of vain and indulgent men who had never had to work hard or fight in their lives.

"Get out of here you filth, you raving lunatic, we have no fear of beating you to death if you threaten us again! Have you any idea what nonsense you are spewing? You're but one man, probably drunk and high and you break in screaming your lungs out, so just turn around and…"

Those were the last words of that young man as he slumped to the floor body limp and now wallowing in its own blood as it poured freely from the hole in his chest. How soft this boy had been, flesh like butter, a creamy texture, but could not hold any strength. It had been too easy for Cain to reach out his hand through the boy's chest and the poor creature was now dead and silenced.

The rest of the group looked on in fear.

A few had started stepping back while the others looked on in anger. You could see the rage knitting the brows of these men who seemed to think themselves, avengers or heroes, as they charged at Cain.

The warm blood dripped off Cain's hand, he raised it to his mouth and lapped at it with his tongue. Young and sweet it tasted. He smiled; this was going to be fun. The next two victims charged, both wishing to strike at Cain who simply sidestepped one grabbing his arm and twisting it till it broke clean off leaving its screaming owner to writhe on the floor. He then used the broken appendage to swipe the other man. It had not been a strong hit, but he had been so shocked by what he had witnessed it was easy to catch him off guard.

As one continued to scream the second had been knocked into a wall dazed and trembling, Cain approached him in ten paces and in that time two victims had been caught, ripping the trembling man's collars and sinking his fangs into their necks. Hot fresh blood of his latest victim poured into Cain's mouth, succulent and rich. This man was in his twenties and had spent his entire time drinking his life away in this opera and yet had never indulged in such other pleasure, like the taste of a woman.

Cain drank deep; it was scarce to find a virgin old enough these days for the blood to taste this sweet. The man on the floor had stopped screaming, but the other members of the group had started to cry or runoff. One brave boy was left; he must have been no more than seventeen, and he lunged at Cain as he fed, hoping to catch him off guard.

"Monster!" he roared.

As he was about to connect, Cain raised a free hand, and the boy stopped just before the outstretched arm.

Cain's nails were only a few millimetres from this youthful face, and the sick child was paralysed. Cain could tell the boy wanted to move but he was caught in a vampire's spell, there was no escape for him. Cain finally released his victim, and the dead man slumped to the floor drained of blood and life. He turned to the boy before him, young and beautiful like many a teenager and so wholly caught in a vampire's power. Cain stepped closer, eyes of wildfire focused on the boy's neck. The boy slowly lifted his arms and undid the collar of his shirt and then the rest of the buttons letting the loose garment fall to the floor. By no means as pale as Yue-ren, he was a lightly coloured thing with the build of many a teenage boy, too young to have developed the muscular physique of a man.

What a delightful treat he would make as the boy bent his neck to one side to allow Cain access and Cain accepted greatly. Again he sank his fangs into the victim before him and drank till all blood and life had been drained away.

Now, Cain thought, the cruellest game of hide and seek lay before him.

Like rats, the others had scattered and hid, but their fear was so full it was easy to sense. Cain rounded corners to see fleeing boys and within a blink of an eye was in front of them as he caught two, one in each hand and squeezed their throats till the breath was crushed out of them. The next was hiding in a study. Cain quietly crept up behind him and in a flash had snapped the man's neck. Some had tried to get the women to safety, but Cain had simply smiled while the group of five females fell into a spell. They turned on the remaining two men beating them with whatever they could find with such unrepressed brutality that Cain had to laugh. Then he beckoned them to him and feasted on two of them, so completely indulged he did not care if his victims were innocents.

What had these women done for him? What had they done for Yue-ren? They were nothing to him, and Cain was insatiable in his rage and hunger.

"Have you girls seen another guest here? If so I very much need you to take me to him," Cain whispered, his voice smooth like fresh blood with a silky texture.

One woman nodded. A maid, one that in recent years had taken to cleaning Selina-ren's most decadent and secret of rooms pointed it out easily. Cain should have realised that of all the rooms in this building that would be the most fitting for Laphiel to be in. He decided to release the three remaining women from his spell and as they came to their senses began to cry and scream.

"We are going to play a game ladies. The first to Selina-ren's most special of guest rooms, the one she did her most private of functions. The first lady there does not get killed tonight. Are you ready? Go!"

Two terrified girls ran. They ran as if hell was opening behind them, but one girl was already in hell screaming like a newborn baby. Cain looked at the pathetic creature. She was neither very pretty nor courageous as she pleaded for her life.

"Please, sir don't kill me. I can offer you anything, anything you want. I know a secret place, a place where Miss Yue-ren hides her jewels. I can give them to you, the most precious and beautiful of jewels. That woman doesn't even appreciate their beauty, but you sir, I bet you would."

It was such a simple bribe, but it made Cain furious. Her life for Yue-ren's jewels? The idea disgusted him.

"Yue-ren does not need to appreciate jewels, you uneducated creature. He is far more precious and beautiful than any bribe you may offer."

Cain sneered as all colour drained from the woman's face and the message in her eyes was clear, 'I'm dead aren't I?'

Cain crushed her throat like a rotten apple core and let the pathetic woman slump to the floor. He then turned and headed to the destined room. With his vampire speed and the ability to glide through the building, he reached the place before his new playmates. Both girls ran up the corridor, so much panic in their eyes, their breath ragged and desperate.

As they arrived, Cain smiled at them and just said, "Looks like I won."

The fear intensified in their eyes as Cain swiped out his claws slashing one's throat as she screamed and died. The last girl remained; the one that had informed him where Laphiel was. He walked up to the shaking woman put a hand on her shoulder slipping down the nightdress she was wearing to expose the flesh of her neck and again bit down. Lavender her blood was like. Fragrant and delicate at the same time, a genuinely floral and pure treat and like all the unfortunate souls that had crossed his path this night she slumped to the floor bloodless and lifeless.

Cain stood for a moment, wiped the blood from his lips and shook the droplets from his hand. He turned to the doors and pushed them open; they had not been locked like the front doorway so opened with ease.

He stepped into the room and looked at the man before him sitting like a self-appointed king and smiled.

"Hello, Laphiel."

"Good evening, Cain."

Chapter 20

THE DOWNFALL OF ACIDIC RAIN

BORED, SO VERY BORED.

That was the feeling Lillith had to deal with this night.

She had wanted to go with Cain, felt sure he needed something to take his frustrations out on. She could most definitely have offered him something to satisfy his lust. Yue-ren, that stupid creature was so fragile like a china doll, and now he was so full of cracks. Was it even worth playing with him? He would never survive Cain, and he would break into tiny pieces so quickly. And yet for some reason, she couldn't follow the vampire off into the night. No, she seemed tied to this place, linked to that worthless person. Cain hadn't been able to see her. Laphiel had kept his word of masking her presence.

All his focus and emotions had been on that china doll he was so obsessed with, but away from Yue-ren with clearer thoughts, Cain would have seen Lillith. It must only be an hour before dawn and Cain had still not returned, and Yue-ren was still fast asleep on the vampire's bed. Luxurious covers caressed the porcelain form of a man whose mind must surely be as broken as his body.

Lillith had enjoyed the torture so much.

To come between them when it looked, they were going to get the release they had both dreamed of was so satisfying. But alas Yue-ren was now haunted by Lillith's presence, and Cain was mad and frustrated and had taken flight into the night. So Lillith was bored, so very bored, staring at the sleeping face of someone she despised was no fun. She longed for him to wake up so she could continue to haunt him. Lillith had put some facts together in the past few hours waiting for Yue-ren to wake up. The reason she was connected to him, how she found him and why she couldn't seem to leave his side was the same reason one heard about in ghost tales. The ghost always came back to haunt the person who killed them.

It was simple; the spirit of the victim comes back from beyond the grave to gain revenge. It becomes a ghost due to unfinished business and Lillith certainly had unfinished business. She had to make Yue-ren suffer and pay for being such a disgusting creature.

Yue-ren was something she couldn't accept. A man pretending to be a woman. Worshipped for being beautiful and talented while no one knew of the person he was underneath it all. Lillith had wanted to expose all that, see Yue-ren fall from his pedestal as people realised he was a pervert, a cross-dressing doll trying to seduce such a beautiful creature as Cain. Laphiel had given her a new life after her death, and although dreams of exposing Yue-ren were out of her reach, she could at least haunt him and drive him mad so he could never get close enough to Cain.

He was bound to wake up soon, it was nearly dawn, and Lillith knew Cain would not return before then. The vampire would have to find refuge somewhere else leaving these two alone in this big old house for Lillith to play her little mind games.

Would day even register in the house of a vampire?

It had so few windows, and the remaining ones were boarded up or had such heavy curtains in front of them. No rogue beams stood a chance of infiltration; this house was an eternal nighttime realm.

Did time even pass in this place where nights just feed into each other?

Lillith could imagine that concepts such as what day of the week it was were invalid in this place. It was a costly and expensive place; Cain had had centuries of wealth to spend making himself a home. In that way not so different from the aristocrats that just lived off the inheritance that had been passed through the generations. A house that echoed of endless night times. A place where pleasure and lust were indulged in and a place where blood was spilt and feasted upon. The home of a vampire. Once Yue-ren was out of the way it was going to be a wonderful life for her. She may be already dead, but that didn't mean she couldn't enjoy her afterlife. An afterlife. What a long time to spend indulging in passions.

The bride of a vampire; two immortal souls spending an eternity of nights embracing and fulfilling their desires.

But first, that china doll. That wretched creature that thought it could find salvation in Cain's arms.

Yue-ren had to be driven out; there was no place in Lillith's dreams for such a perversion. Lillith had a day to drive him mad, to drive him out and ultimately drive him to death. After all, Yue-ren had killed her so it was only fair that she would be the instrument in his death. It was then she felt it a small pain in her chest, in fact, pain from the scar on her body, a knife scar. Why all of a sudden was it hurting? Her chest felt tight. Something inside was squeezing, and the pain from her scar was sharp. It had only started to hurt when she contemplated Yue-ren's suicide.

In a single moment, it fell into place the one threat that demon Laphiel had made.

"You may torture that alabaster beauty, break his mind, ruin him completely but if you go so far as for him to commit suicide, then our deal is void."

That was right, she wasn't allowed to let Yue-ren commit suicide otherwise her new life would be forfeited.

Laphiel had made it clear that the contract they shared, him giving her new life, powers and a chance to gain the thing she wanted and desired would become void if she broke one rule. The rule was Yue-ren had to live and as much as she had hated that, she knew that death would have been an easy escape compared to a life that belonged to a demon. If she broke the contract, she was dead too, but it seemed the demon was even stricter than that, it seemed that even if she thought of killing Yue-ren, it was breaching the contract. The pain in her scar was intense. She had to quell her hatred and wish of death on Yue-ren. She had the power to drive him away; there was no need to kill him. She didn't want this pain in her chest. No, she had no desire to suffer, be damned with Yue-ren's fate.

She only wanted one thing - Cain.

Let the demon have what he wanted.

The pain began to lessen as she assured her scar that killing Yue-ren was far from her mind.

As Lillith composed herself, she wondered why immortal beings such as those two were so obsessed with that lithe man.

Why such attraction to someone? Especially someone whose existence was a lie.

Had they both been lusting over Yue-ren believing him to be a woman? Did they both know he was male? Did it even matter to them? Did his androgynous beauty tran- scend such notions? What was so perfect and desirable about that creature? Was it only Yue-ren's appearance they were attracted to? Did it not matter if he was male or female or was there something in his tortured soul they found beautiful? Wouldn't such dark and twisted creatures as a vampire and a demon naturally fall for the most tormented human they found? Cain surely knew Yue-ren was male. She could see it in his eyes, understanding, knowledge and lust. His sex had not mattered.

As for Laphiel, he would not have cared, all humans were the same to him, playthings.

As Lillith pondered these thoughts something caught her attention. A figure stirring, eyes fluttering open registering its surrounding and for a moment comfort and familiarity registering on its pale features. Yue-ren was just lying there, the sheets around his body being pulled up to his face, the scent from the sheets registering and bringing comfort as a soft smile spread on his lips.

This was no good, Lillith would have to correct this, make sure that not even for a moment did Yue-ren feel safe. As softly and as effortlessly as she could Lillith lay down on the bed behind Yue-ren a couple of inches from his back and then blew softly on his neck causing delicate white hairs to flutter slightly. Yue-ren turned in the bed, as inevitable that it was Cain behind as Lillith was that it was not. He turned to face the person sharing this bed, the covers pulling tightly against him until he was facing the red-headed women whose hair had spilt across the pillow like rivers of blood and eyes fixed on his.

What an amusing site this was as all comfort drained from those delicate androgynous features. Eyes glazing over slightly as realisation could be read in them. Shock and fear replaced all other emotions, his eyes widening as the horror sunk in.

She was still there.

"Morning beautiful, miss me?"

She smiled warmly though her eyes betrayed all the mischief and malice she was thinking at the time. Lillith loved this. Yue-ren's lips had parted, but he was torn between screaming again or just gaping like a fish.

To Lilith's disappointment, he tried to compose himself and tried to mouth out the word, "Why?"

"Why my pretty boy? Don't you know? Ghosts always haunt those that kill them. Ah, did you think it had been some horrible dream, and you were safe with your vampire lover? Sorry precious, but he's out. It's just you and me so don't look so shocked."

Lillith reached out a hand and stroked his check; pale and unblemished, his spilt tears had dried leaving nothing but perfect milky skin to the touch.

"I'm not leaving you. I have a duty to perform. I have to make sure you leave Cain because something as perverse as you doesn't deserve such a magnificent creature."

With this he slapped her hand away, anger marring those delicate features.

He tried to push himself off the bed only to fight embarrassingly with the cover he had entwined himself in. After a flustered show, he was finally on his feet backing away from the bed, embarrassed that he had to fight with his own covers, angry at the woman lying there and scared that he was alone with a phantom that was undoubtedly trying to drive him mad.

"Leave!" His voice was shaky and unconvincing. This man had never really demanded anything in his life.

Did he even understand how weak he sounded?

"I… I deserve to be here, this is where I belong. It's you that needs…that needs to be driven out."

He was scared. His hand clenched into a fist, nails

digging into the soft, delicate palms of his hands and at any moment they were likely to draw blood.

"No, how exactly do you think you belong here? After all, you're a liar, a fake, a fraud and not to mention a murderer. Oh, and how about a perversion as well as a broken china doll? Frail, weak and simply pathetic. You haven't done a thing to redeem any of that. You're not even a very good person. Instead of making up for your crimes, for your lies, you run away and hide, you seek salvation."

Lillith had risen from the bed as she spoke.

It look liked gliding as she slowly moved towards Yue-ren. A haunting sight, a vengeful ghost, hair as red as blood spilling into the night and eyes so bright they almost glowed in the darkness. There was no breeze in the room, but her hair swayed about her as she advanced. Lillith would never get tired of these words; never get bored of telling this useless excuse of a human what she thought of him and exactly why he didn't deserve anything. He really did deserve to die...Pain shot through the scar in her chest, sharp like the knife had never been taken out. 'Shit!' she thought, closing her eyes briefly trying to regain herself and to let thoughts of Yue-ren's death fade from her mind.

It was in this moment that Yue-ren saw an opening, a chance, a single moment of time where he could only do one thing, run.

And so he did.

He took this chance and ran for the bedroom door. He needed to get away, think and escape. He was getting tired of running, of being abused and tortured. Cain must have headed out into the night to take out his frustration on someone. If he found him, he could convince him that this phantom was real and that he needed Cain's strength so he could face this obstacle.

"YUE-REN!"

Lillith had regained herself and fuelled by anger she had started after Yue-ren determined to give him no peace, no escape from her torment.

"There's nowhere you can run from me. Cain will never be a comfort to you, and he will be mine!"

Lillith screamed through the corridors, screamed her vile abuse and with each passing word Yue-ren slowed as if physically weakening. Her foul tongue and cruel words were taking their toll on him. Yue-ren's spirit was breaking.

He ran out of the corridor onto a landing, the balcony that connected one side of the house to another.

If he ran forward, he would simply be lost in more mazes of Cain's night palace, but this balcony was also where the grand stairs were. These stairs led down, and he could even see the front door from them. All he had to do was make a right turn into the entrance foyer and then out through the doors into the night. But as he ran out onto the balcony, Lillith was there in front of him just smiling at him. So taken back by the shock that she was now in front of him he stumbled and tripped.

Lillith began to laugh, high pitched and mocking as the lithe beauty rolled down the staircase to the bottom landing on the cold ground beneath.

How embarrassing that the graceful beauty Yue-ren just tumbled down a staircase, if only someone else had seen this humiliation. Yue-ren was lying at the bottom of the stairs. Lillith knew the fall hadn't killed him for there was no ache in her chest, no pressing knife wound to her breast. She walked down the stairs still laughing at the spilt mess on the floor, like a pool of milk spilt on the floor. This was not a delicate and dignified view of the so admired opera star.

"Oh dear look at you. How embarrassing. What happened to all your grace?"

"SHUT UP! SHUT UP!"

"Oh don't be so snappy, oh poor little boy. Are you crying again? My my, you do love to cry don't you?"

Yue-ren lay there trying to draw in breaths.

He was tired, weak and drained both emotionally and physically. He was trying to hold back more tears. Why was this happening to him? Why was he not free of torture, pain and misery?

Where was Cain?

Then a face appeared to him, one of a forgotten place, of a time he had truly lived. The face of a young girl who had never judged him and a family that had comforted him and given him freedom. Annabel. Hadn't she encouraged him to live a life for himself and not to fear his weaknesses? Wherever this sweet girl rested now, her family had been true and good, and he couldn't disgrace their memory by acting like a coddled child. No, he couldn't always rely on the vampire, if he learnt nothing of his strength then this ghost was right, he was pathetic. For once in his wretched life, he had to fight back, he had to fight he had to earn the right to the happiness and pleasures he wished for. Cain was out there in the night fighting, killing and all because he was frustrated with Yue-ren. But was that all? What was this feeling that was growing as he lay on the floor?

Yue-ren couldn't understand, but something inside told him there was more to Cain's absence.

"Are we going to just lie on the floor all day? Come on precious, get up now. I was having fun playing chase, you really need more exercise."

Lillith was about to go into another barrage of verbal abuse, another dialogue of why Yue-ren was pathetic and worthless when he began to stir. He pushed himself up with his arms and then onto his knees. He grabbed the bottom railing of the stairs to hoist himself onto his feet.

The palms of his hands were bleeding, from the small

wounds his nails had made earlier, a small trickle of blood was running its course down his arms, and now that he was standing it ran the other way making small blood trails over his pale skin. His legs looked bruised but not broken, and there was a dark bruise across his face.

"Oh dear, look at your pretty face, it's all bruised! How unfortunate you look..."

"Enough! I won't listen to you anymore. There... there's somewhere I have to be...someone I have to see. He needs me. I don't have time to play with you so hold your tongue!"

Yue-ren was panting, but his voice wasn't as shaky as before. There was more conviction behind his words, more force and determination than Lillith had ever heard before coming from this delicate creature.

"Ignorant boy. Don't you dare speak to me like that! You killed me, remember? I have all the right in the world to torture you, so you better listen to me. You better not ignore me, you have to listen to me, you have to..."

But Yue-ren wasn't listening. Something else was pressing him. He needed to go somewhere else; he needed to go to the Opera House. He walked to the front doors turning the latch and pushing them wide open. It took a moment to adjust; he had been lying in darkness for a while so that at first the light hurt his eyes. He blinked, shielding his eyes from the sun's rays. It was dawn, and a clear sky meant the sun bathed him in its early light.

He adjusted and took a step out into the waking world, warm and bright.

Perhaps this is the last chance I'll see the morning world, he thought to himself. He had to go to Cain and once there make sure they were never parted again.

"NOOOO! Come back and listen to me! Listen to me! LISTEN TO ME!"

But Lilith's words were wasted; Yue-ren was walking into the bright world with some unknown strength, some new determination. Something was more important to him than his own body, mind or sanity and she had lost her power over him.

The last thing Yue-ren heard was an ear piercing scream, a scream so vile and tortured that it made him shiver. Lilith's voice rang out into the dawn, but no one would respond to it; the only person that was able to see or hear her was Yue-ren and he was gone.

She stood in the doorway, tears rolling down her face; throat so sore it was like she had screamed out needles and all the time a squeezing sensation in her chest and a knife wound that felt like new.

Chapter 21

Laphel

THE TEMPEST OF SUN AND STORM

THE ROOM FELT HOT AS IF IT WAS PACKED WITH BODIES all trying to compete for space and oxygen but instead giving off heat and making the air thin.

It was only the two of them staring at each other both wearing a look of conceit, smugness and that look of joy only those that felt joy in killing and harm could wear. They were creatures not of the human world, each was violent and dangerous and equally passionate and powerful, and both these creatures knew this.

The room felt like it trembled, the heavy air vibrating to some unseen force the walls pulsating as if they stood inside the belly of some great beast and yet there was no movement. It was silent; they had no words for each other there was no need, there was only the desire for destruction, revenge and dominance. Only one of these creatures was going to walk away from this encounter, vampire or demon. The faint sound of a hum mixed with the deep breaths of these two enemies made the very air feel alive and thirsty, thirsty for violence and blood. It was like anticipation was hanging off the walls, each drape or curtain soaked in it.

Both men knew that the first move could decide the fate of a battle, so they stood to face each other trying to anticipate each other while the room attempted to hold its breath and bear the weight. Time had stood still for them, beasts as ancient as these could wait for years to strike, suns could rise and fall before even a strike was made, but the anticipation was half the fun in battle.

The anticipation grew too much for the room even the air could not wait and the tremor that it was carrying began to show signs.

It was like gravity itself was fighting with all the unseen forces of the night, neither men had even had to move to cause the effects that were beginning to show. First little cracks in the walls, shards of the wall crumbling or peeling. The pictures started to tremble, their glass cracking and splitting, in one corner a vase tumbled from its resting place, smashing into pieces on the waiting floor. Even the floors seem to pulse as if trying to consume the small objects that were tumbling to it.

This was what it meant for creatures of the night to face each other, not bound by the rules of human society their very presence could affect the space they inhabited. The very moisture in the air began to gather and form droplets and then as if slow motion fall to the ground as if afraid to land. Once it landed it did not rest, it trickled into small pools around Cain's feet swirling in small circles, in patches around him waiting for some signal that they were for some purposes.

"And so we face each other at last".

"Cool your tongue demon; this isn't the time for words we have nothing to say to each other".

Cain spoke with confidence and grace but underneath his words were restrained, he wanted to use more venom in his words, he wanted to use something more primal than the pleasant speech of gentlemen for both of them knew that neither was a gentleman.

"True vampire, we have no need for human words or voices, let it begin".

And as if the room had finally let out the breath it was keeping, the walls and floor knew to stop retraining itself, and there was no need to tremor in anticipation they all screamed out together.

As if a hurricane had been trapped indoors, every item in the room was ripped from its place and tossed into a vortex of chaos and power. All at once the glass in the room smashed, sending sharp and cutting rain into the storm. The droplets of water lifted themselves from the floor and took the shape of spheres as they gathered speed in their spiral dance.

And all along as this storm crashed about them, two figures stood still and unmoved neither afraid nor threatened, neither affected to the chaos they stood in and both smiling to each other.

Laphiel looked into the vortex and smiled, raising a single hand toward the sight before him and watched as crystals of glass began to dance around his outstretched palm.

As more collected, they began to glow, become hot and red and take of the form they were before they set as glass. The warm, sharp liquid pulsated and danced waiting for its instruction and with a click of his fingers Laphiel gave the command, and it hurled itself at the figure before it. In an instant, super-heated glass cut through the storm towards Cain, who stood unmoved as in a blink of an eye the molten weapon was engulfed by a sphere or water. Cain smirked, and Laphiel sneered as the sphere of water formed a circle around Cain.

Laphiel knew that each molten shot he made would be

engulfed by the watery defence Cain had secured. Cain knew there was no time to think about his small victory and in an instant, the spheres of water formed balls of ice and shot through the room. Laphiel jumped out of the way, and the frozen balls tore through the wall that had been behind him.

The room pulsated once more and shuddered as another attack was launched molten sphere met frozen sphere, and on the impact a great wall of steam filled the room leaving both men blind to each other's movement.

Cain could hear Laphiel and Laphiel could sense Cain, and even though they now were enclosed in a maze of steam and spinning debris spheres of hot and cold still collided with each other until an almighty crash and the sound of stone, wood and metal supports falling was heard. The entire storm was sucked out into the night losing its velocity and spilling its contents into the courtyard that had been crashed into. All at once the steam was lifted, and both Cain and Laphiel realised that their weapons had smashed through an outer wall. They looked at each other and would have laughed if this was not a battle and a quest for a kill.

It was time to stop playing silly games and take this fight more seriously, they knew to throw spheres at each other was a waste of time.

It was dusk out in the world, they had waited nearly a full day before blows had been struck and the fading sunburned at Cain, not strong enough to combust him but enough to slow him down.

He would have to hope that Laphiel's pride and love to torture would prolong this fight until proper darkness descended. But Demons are vain things and will always play first and kill later so the lowering sun at Cain's back would be a minor nuisance until it faded and he was free to use all the powers at his command.

Laphiel summoned all the debris in sight, the furniture, the now destroyed wall and anything else that had been ripped into this battle, creating a giant sphere and hurled at Cain; as Cain prepared to defend it, he followed close behind to make his sneak attack. The figure emerged through the sphere, at first like a cloud of smoke and then the mist to shape and Cain was thereupon Laphiel, his hands tightly on his shoulders pushing him back into whatever surface he chose to slam their bodies into.

The shock had caused the ball of debris to lose focus, and it fell to the ground scorching and melting the surface below it.

Cain let out a primal scream as he pushed the demon back and in return, Laphiel opened his mouth as if to scream, but instead, a cloud of gas came out that smelt of sulphur and burned like the fires of hell this demon was probably born in. Immediately Cain let go and put his hands to his face, and he felt the acidic gas melt his skin and features.

Laphiel took this chance to halt himself from the force of being pushed back and from the spot where his sphere had fallen, his weapon a pit of hot tar, he reforged it into chains that shot out and wrapped at Cain's body. The tar pit itself burned a deep hole, and only blackness could be seen in its depths as the chains crawl up from this dark wound. Laphiel laughed,

"Did you forget I am a demon? I have the very powers of hell at my command! You are just a creature that is destined to walk among humans for all time, you can't compete, but don't worry I will send you to hell."

The chains around Cain's body tightened and tore at his flesh as he was pulled into the pit they had come from. Already the flesh of Cain's face began to heal, and even though the chains were ripping through his clothes and flesh, he did not worry. He looked at Laphiel and smiled,

"And did you forget I am one of the oldest vampires left, a true master vampire you ignorant fool".

With that, his body burst into a swarm of dark shapes each one with glowing eyes and a taste for blood.

The swarm of bats flew high into the sky and chains fell to the ground as Laphiel looked up. Before he could curse himself for forgetting about a master vampires abilities, the swarm of bats descended on him, a hundred claws and teeth attacking every inch of him as he screamed out in pain, as his flesh was ripped away from him. It took all his concentration not to wave his arms about in panic like a stupid human and as his anger grew, and so did his rage, his body burned. Soon his temperature was beyond anything a human could withstand, and his body was consumed in blazing flame.

The screech of the bats would have deafened any creature that had heard it, as the swarm fell to the ground trying to save their burning wings. Laphiel's body burned on till his clothes and hair had turned to cinder and then his flesh. As the bats reformed their original shape Cain took heavy breaths, his body was severely burned, and he was bleeding all over he could feel blood hot and thick on his face as he looked up.

The figure of Laphiel burned on until there was nothing left to burn and the flame died, and the figure was nothing but ash that was swept into the night air until the only reminder of Laphiel was the smell of his own burnt body.

"Had he sacrificed his life to destroy me, was that his last and fatal stand?"

Even as he said these words, a faint voice was heard, and a figure approached from the wreckage of the opera house.

"Cain."

It was barely a whisper, but Cain knew who owned the voice, and as he looked up, it was like the moon had fallen from the sky taken form and was walking towards him.

"Yue-ren"

Cain outstretched his arm, and Yue-ren ran to him, tears in his eyes falling into his embrace. Whatever pain Cain's body was in didn't matter, it would heal soon enough, and he had his beloved in his arms. Cain was weak and badly wounded as the two slumped to the floor Yue-ren pulling Cain into a seated embrace. Cain could feel his energy fade as his body tried to heal itself, and so they sat regarding the destruction around them.

Cain's head was in Yue-ren's lap enjoying the comfort, and listening gently as Yue-ren hummed one of his old opera house songs. The world was peaceful, and they were together.

"So the prodigal son has returned, at last, we are reunited my lovely Yue-ren."

Cain's eyes that had been closed snapped open staring into the darkness searching out his enemy's voice.

"Where are you demon? Show yourself?"

"Unfortunately I'm not really in any fit shape at the moment, which I suppose is lucky for you otherwise I would simply walk off with my pretty boy with you too weak to stop me."

"Cain, what is he talking of? What is this voice and why does it make me feel sick and disgusting? Isn't it over? Aren't we free? Why am I trembling, why?"

"So you haven't even told the boy, tut, tut Mr Vampire, keeping secrets. Every child deserves to know who their father is. Well, Yue-ren many years ago I was your mother's lover, and her being such a whore couldn't get enough of me, and well one thing led to another and then one day you were born. So you see my dear you're the son of a whore and a demon."

"NO! don't lie you've been trying to mess with my head, sending ghosts to drive me mad, this is just another trick a lie, a hateful lie, Cain, say it isn't the truth."

But even as Yue-ren looked at Cain he could sense that this was not all lies, a demon, a foul demon and probably the one responsible for so much torture in his life so much pain. A sick feeling was in Yue-ren's gut like some ugly truth wanted to be vomited free. But he had decided his pathetic self-loathing was to end, hadn't he come here determined to not fall over his own feet and live free regardless.

He wasn't going to let anyone dictate who he was or change his new found courage.

"So what demon, you're weak, you said it yourself, and soon Cain will be healed, and then he will destroy you, I knew I was wretched from the beginning, I could think such things. Well if I am the son of a demon and a whore then so be it, I'm tired of being tortured and used, I am not as weak as you think anymore."

"Oh, what backbone my little beauty has developed; well we can't have that, and oh look someone else has come to join the party and she doesn't seem to be in a very good mode at all, dear oh dear. How about you let daddy go heal up, and you play with your new friend. Oh and Cain since you're so old and all maybe you should have a little nap, rest will do you good and let the kids catch up as well."

Laphiel's presence vanished; Cain tried to follow it but his body ached, and he was using his concentration to heal still burnt flesh and stop his blood from flowing away. He looked at Yue-ren and all of a sudden he grew worried. His beauty, his love, he had never seen such a look on his face.

Yue-ren was looking away from them, his features twisted and wild.

It was pure hatred, pure anger, contempt and disgust, a look so vile even Cain had to break his gaze from him and look at the creature that had earned such a look.

Chapter 22

THE FADING OF THE RAIN

EVEN GREAT BEAUTY COULD LOOK UGLY, FEATURES polluted by hatred and anger could rot such a lovely face.

Eyes that once would have taken a person's breath away could ooze such contempt and malice, how amusing. Yet at the same time, the look was shared, for she could not derive pleasure from seeing such beauty contort into such ugliness no Lillith had other things to plague her. Worse was the very fact she had known Laphiel had been fighting he had been the one that had given her life she knew they were connected it was his blood, his demonic power that had given her.

What worried her was that he had apparently been dealt a severe blow for she had gotten weaker. She had felt some of her growing weak, she had felt like the smoke of a candle, strong while it burns, then just after it is put out stronger still for the smoke is the only reminder that the candle burned but then even this reminder this shadow of what once was fades. Could it be if Laphiel died she would also cease to exist? Was she so dependent on him?

No, Lillith had things to do and first was destroy Yue-ren and his hating vile eyes.

As Laphiel had vanished to recover his strength she had felt that sudden increase in her own existence, that reassurance that she was part him, she was now the smoke of a newly extinguished flame and for this moment she had strength.

She had no idea how much or how long it would last once Laphiel recovered she would just be the dark shadow of his power, but for now she was strong. And be damned if she wasn't going to use that strength, she may have sworn not to harm Yue-ren or Laphiel would destroy her but now he was weak and recovering how could he stop her? With Yue-ren cradling the man she wanted in his arms she couldn't hold herself back anymore. This was it if she died so be it but she would damn that porcelain doll that ruined everything for her.

She would kill Yue-ren she would have revenge.

As her will increased she felt the heat inside her, she felt blood and flesh, and she knew she had regained a measure of her corporeal existence.

Lillith knew it was now or never, time to take one last leap, use all the physical strength left in her and tear that useless creature away, she wanted to put her hand to his neck and squeeze the life out of him. She could do this, the only people to stop her were weak and recovering. She could see Cain looking at her, his eyes grew large at first when he realised her form had crawled its way back into existence and now realisation had settled over his handsome features. He knew he didn't have to ask, he knew it had been her ghost haunting Yue-ren, driving him mad and denying Cain what he wanted.

He also hated her for that, but behind his hateful and cold mask was frustration for he knew that he had no power at this moment and could not stop her, no, this moment was hers, and it was all going to end now, it was over everything. Even the knife wound that pulsated and burned only fuelled her made her stronger and made this moment possible.

"Yue-ren!"

Lillith screamed the world slowed, each step she took as she ran felt like slow motion.

Her feet landed on the floor heavily allowing small clouds of dust to be thrown back, as she raised her foot dirt scattered behind her. Sound no longer existed, all was silence but the beating of her heart loud and strong causing blood to rush and pump hot and vicious. Her eyes were wild like a caged beast tortured and angered until at last a chance was made for its attack, for its moment. Yue-ren stood, his clothes and hair lightly waving in the night's air, a single strand across his face, the slight glow of a tear in the corner of his eye but not a tear of sorrow one of anger. In his eyes, a look of resignation, of a man that had made up his mind even as Cain's blood had patterned his clothes he still looked determined.

Cain lay there on the ground blood drying about him, his face complete concentration as if thinking, "another moment, another moment and I can heal enough to stop", this but it was Lilith's moment as she outstretched her hands for Yue-ren's neck her finders itching to feel his last breath escape and then the moment came.

The world stopped, Yue-ren a picture of determination, anger and decision, his eyes never looked more focused, no fear at all just understanding as if he finally understood now what was going to happen, as if he finally accepted his fate and no longer feared the moment.

But the moment had changed in that very last fraction of a second, in all of fates cruelty and irony as if all imagination, destiny, desire, understanding as if all the forces of the earth at one instance had cried in one voice, "No!" Every authority in unison had agreed and had sung together to make their wish truth, and their desire was not Lilith's.

This was not her moment, she had been judged and tried and time and existence had deemed her moment over and had given Yue-ren his. So close, her fingers had been so close, but as they reached their target, they had splintered and cracked. Like a mirror that was dropped, her hand shattered like glass, shards of which flew back at her tearing through flesh ripping into her face. Her very flesh unravelled, her blood and heat burning off into nothingness and every muscle tearing and ripping itself free from her body.

The pain was immense, her very corporeal existence being destroyed leaving her with only the smoke, just the shadow of Laphiel's power. And as her spirit form waived she looked at Yue-ren, and he had never looked more alive, more brilliant and powerful. It as was if he glowed, though not a pure, no nothing so angelic, this was a dark glow, a red-tinted flame seemed to dance across his features, his blood almost visible in the veins underneath his skin as if his blood was molten like magma.

Cain began to rise until he stood behind Yue-ren and placed a hand on his shoulder. You could tell the contact was hot from the slight vibrations in the air and as if hot and cold had collided, a very faint mist writhed from the contact zone.

"What, oh god, what is this, how could this happen, you monsters, what the hell are you doing to me?"

Lillith shouted, her voice hoarse and pained and it was Cain that answered.

"I am not doing anything to you, this is Yue-ren's power this is his true self so buried even I didn't know it existed.

But it seems you have pushed him so far that he has learnt to fight back, so in fact it's your fault that this power was released, so I suppose I have to thank you for it."

Lillith couldn't understand her body was gone, she was indeed a ghost just a whisper in time and space. Yue-ren seemed to quiet the rage, and the force his body emitted died away until he looked normal and almost sad.

"I don't completely understand it, I wish Laphiel hadn't created you, but I can not undo it. You are tied to his blood, and until his blood is destroyed, you will not be extinguished. Even I feel sorrow for what you have become, you are a ghost, but I have no fear of you, and if you ever come near us again, I will rip as much of your existence out of this world as I can."

"I still don't get it, how do you have power? You're weak, false, pathetic and a disgusting excuse for a human. How can you hold any power over me?"

But Yue-ren wasn't listening, he had turned away to look into the distance, a faint glow appearing on the horizon, the day was coming. Cain stepped up towards him, wrapping them together ready to disappear into the dawn. But before they did, he said one last thing.

"So caught up in yourself you didn't see anything else. Laphiel used you to drive Yue-ren to him. Laphiel's blood created you and bound you but if you had listened to how Yue-ren came to be you would have understood where Yue-ren got his power. You shared abound not only with a demon but the child of that demon, you share with the man you hate more than anything in this life, and you have allowed yourself to be destroyed by this. Laphiel has no use for you; Yue-ren does not fear you, and I couldn't care less about you. Goodbye, dear ghost enjoy your eternity."

Cain said the last words with a smile before pulling Yue-ren closer to him, and they both rose into the awakening dawn travelling the rooftops until they disappeared from view. Lillith just stood there, watching dawns light slowly illuminate the world, casting light on the wreckage of the opera house, waiting as the beams shown through her body as if she wasn't even there.

Nothing, she was really nothing. She was just a ghost

Chapter 23

Cain

AND THE SUN EMBRACES MOON

DAWN WAS UNDERWAY IN THE WORLD BRINGING ALL THE light, warmth and movement of the day but this was no concern to two figures still wrapped in darkness.

They had arrived before the light was up, shed their clothes and concerns and now rested in each other's arms in the comfort and warmth of Cain's bed. Cain's body had healed, the last remnant of burns and battle gone from his skin while Yue-ren's mind had found a new place to dwell away from the harsh and vicious world.

Neither cared about anything else but each other, both had been through enough to know that the time for running, hating, fear, anger and confrontation was over. It was about themselves and this very moment. Cain and Yue-ren were both naked beneath the sheets, their warm bodies pressed against each other, perfect flesh against perfect flesh. Yue-ren was tucked beneath Cain's chin, his face resting in the crook of Cain's neck.

Cain could feel hot breath against his neck, just like Yue-ren could smell Cain's scent: a mixture of darkness, power and warm blood. It was an intoxicating smell like forbidden desires, no wonder the vampire was such a crea-ture of lust, his very body invited such passion and wanting. Cain could sense Yue-ren's growing arousal; he could almost taste the lust rising in his lover's body.

With that knowledge, his own desire and need grew, and he bent his head down and locked eyes with the object of so much passion, want, need and desire. Their lips met, a kiss so full of force and strength it could have sucked the very soul out of a weaker man. But neither of them were weak, both had their strength and passion. The kiss was like fire, it was like blood, rich and robust and it burned with fury and delight.

This kiss was more potent than either could have imagined, both clinging on to each other so Yue-ren could feel Cain's nails claiming the flesh on his back and he felt alive.

After an eternity of fire and lust, they broke the kiss, Yue-ren panting heavily trying to gulp down air, his head dizzy eyes unfocused.

Through the haze of need and desire, he could see Cain's brilliant eyes shine at him, amber orbs of pure want. Cain moved in to kiss again this time his lips falling on Yue-ren's collarbone, hot claiming kisses devouring Yue-ren's body. Cain pushed Yue-ren into the bed, his weight on top of the exquisite man he now had beneath him. The man whose eyes were tightly shut and whose breaths were heavy and full. Yue-ren's hands had found fistfuls of bedding to grasp onto holding on with all his might in case he should fall.

Cain continued to claim, to devour, kisses trailing done torso to stomach and then with one hand he lifted a slender leg and kissed the flesh beneath Yue-ren's thigh.

Yue-ren's voice was high as he moaned into the night, the blush across his face so full of hot blood. He could feel

Cain's strong hands one tightly clamped to his leg, the other his hip.

Cain must have been kneeling to gain such access to Yue-ren's thigh as tongue and teeth played with the sensitive flesh working their way to where Yue-ren's need grew hot and moist.

Yue-ren had never been so painfully aroused, he had never felt so wanting; so full and hot only to be driven more lustful by the hot breaths upon his arousal.

Cain's eye filled with delight as he took Yue-ren into his mouth, engulfing all the desire Yue-ren had for him. Cain's hand still kept Yue-ren's hip pressed into the bed while the other had pushed Yue-ren's leg back, so his knee almost touched his shoulder.

He sucked strong and hard then relaxed to trail his teeth down Yue-ren's length. Yue-ren shouted to the night, moaned in pleasure and delight holding back nothing of his desire, his hands moving from the bed covers into Cain's hair, roughly grasping at the blond locks. Cain gently let the still aroused length fall from his mouth, a hiss of disappointment escaped Yue-ren's lips which made Cain laugh.

Cain lapped at the head, teasing little licks that inspired small mews from Yue-ren, he did the same up the length occasionally moving to kiss the tip or pelvic bone or sensitive skin of the thigh, and when he thought Yue-ren could take the teasing no more, he once again took the length into his mouth. Slowly, with painful precision he let his teeth slide up it, making sure his lips did not touch Yue-ren's length.

Yue-ren's breaths were ragged and sharp the only word he could form and give life to was, "Please".

At this Cain smiled, allowing his lips to taste the warm flesh in his mouth as he devoured the flavour.

Yue-ren tossed his head back, his hands and nails

digging into the scalp of Cain's head and he let out a passionate scream before releasing himself into Cain's mouth.

Cain, well prepared for this, swallowed all the salty flavour, drinking Yue-ren's very essence down before letting him slip from his mouth, giving the tip a final kiss before looking at Yue-ren's flushed and sweaty features.

Yue-ren's eyes were half open, trying to stare up at him, both hands laid by his side beads of sweat dotting his body as Cain lapped up some of the sweat that had pooled in Yue-ren's belly button. What a sight to have finally gotten the object of all his emotions, wants and needs, to have Yue-ren flushed, sweating and wanting beneath him.

Cain became painfully aware of his own need, his own arousal hot and heavy. He leaned in to kiss Yue-ren again, their bodies flushed against each other, Cain allowing Yue-ren's leg to drop so he could bring his hand up and grasped the face of the man he desired so. Yue-ren could feel Cain's desire and need pushing against his, the contact so maddeningly hot as the hand that had come to cup his face began to travel low again.

Reaching between his legs, he started to coax life back into Yue-ren's soft length. After a few gentle strokes it began to strengthen once more that Cain's hand moved away he allowed for both lengths to press and rub against each other until both men were thoroughly aroused and filled with lust. Yue-ren had kept his foot on the bed, so his leg was bent rather than rested, but as Cain had stroked him, both legs had risen until they were wrapped around Cain's waist, feet resting on the small of his back.

Cain himself could no longer keep quiet low moans like liquid dark need echoed from his lips, and he knew what he wanted now more than anything.

The hand that was clamped to hip had already started to

leave marks, small welts where fingernails dug in and the sign of bruising on the pure white flesh. He needed this hand to stay there to keep Yue-ren steady so as not to hurt him, as well as to support himself so as to not lose himself in his own lusts and passions. Again he kneeled, breaking the contact and causing Yue-ren to hiss at the loss and tighten the grips of his legs as well wrap both arms around Cain's neck burying his face in Cain's hair.

His free hand slid to that soft, beautiful and delicate area of skin under the thigh, and he took a sharp nail and drew a cut across it. Yue-ren winced slightly at the pain but so lost in lust and need he put the thought of pain to the back of his mind. The cut was not too deep, but enough that drops of ruby blood fell from the wound onto the awaiting hand. When a small pool had formed, he licked the wound so that it would heal and lowered his fingers, so the drops trickled down and coated the awaiting fingers. He bought this to Yue-ren's back and then lower, trailing on finger down until he found the entrance he was searching for.

Yue-ren stiffened slightly, a moment of fear as he began to comprehend what was about to happen he steadied himself as he wanted this as much as Cain.

Cain teased the small round opening with his middle finger just trailing around the ring of muscle that guarded the entrance before allowing his finger to slip past this guard.

Slowly he moved this finger back and forth until Yue-ren had relaxed to this new sensation and grew more accepting.

When Cain felt this was so, he pushed a little deeper and found Yue-ren's body to already be accepting, so he added another finger repeating the motion until he had three fingers working. Yue-ren winced at first, his arms tight around Cain's neck, his legs tightly clamped, trying to get used to the sensation of something opening and massaging him from the inside.

His breaths were heavy and his moans loud and full of lust and again he found his voice for a moment to allow his lips to form words and ask, "More".

Cain knew Yue-ren was prepared; there was nothing more he could do. He wanted a far more satisfying experience, he wanted ultimate pleasure, and he wanted to share it with the man pressed so wantonly against him.

He slowly moved the probing, massaging and searching digits from Yue-ren and positioned himself; his own arousal almost painful with want and anticipation.

"Are you ready?"

He felt Yue-ren nod, the ability to form words lost to their lustful dance, and so he entered his arousal, pushing past the guarded muscle ring into the hot a tight cavern of Yue-ren's waiting body.

Yue-ren gave a scream, half pained, half wanting and then bit down, his teeth sinking into Cain's shoulder and slightly breaking the flesh. His whole body shaking with the experience, tears forming at the corner of his eyes, his mind trying to grip onto how one could feel so filled and yet also wanting more.

Cain slowly pushed until his entire length was inside Yue-ren, a deep dark moan straining out of his throat. Hot, tight, possessive and exquisite, it took all his self-control to not completely devour this body before him. Slowly he pulled back, taking his time; a little back, a little in, getting to feel the sensation that Yue-ren clamped around him and allow his beauty to get used to the new experience.

Setting a slow and gentle rhythm, until Yue-ren stopped biting and allowed for moans of delight to escape his lips. Seeing Yue-ren relax into Cain movements, he began to lessen his control a little so he could fully pleasure both bodies. His pace increased and so did the strengths of his thrusts strong and deep until Yue-ren lost his grip and again was holding onto the covers his voice ringing into the night with ecstasy.

Cain released Yue-ren's pinned body allowing him to match the thrusts with his own and letting his own hands push both Yue-ren's legs over his shoulders to increase the depth of his thrusts until he hit the spot, a deep and secret place that made Yue-ren scream with all his passions.

Yue-ren's eyes snapped open the look of lust, love and sheer ecstasy apparent across his features as their eyes locked.

Cain's thrust again, Yue-ren screamed, and Cain tossed his head back letting his own howl of delight out, his golden hair spilling back. Yue-ren used his strength and pushed up with his arms. Cain, sensing the movement, looked back and wrapped his around Yue-ren's waist pulling him to him until Yue-ren was sitting on him, his arousal so deep within Yue-ren's body.

They kissed passionate and raw, Yue-ren's hands tangled in Cain's hair, their lips fierce upon each other while Cain's remaining free hand again went to stroke and pump Yue-ren's aching arousal. They were like something wild devouring each other and riding a storm of lust until Yue-ren's body could take no more.

Cain thrust upwards again, hitting that secret spot and releasing all his passion.

His head rolling back while Cain supported his body, so it didn't collapse with exhaustion. He felt everything go hot and tight as his release caused him to clamp down on Cain even more.

With one final thrust, Cain released into Yue-ren's body, hot liquid filling him and the howl like midnight echoing through the room. Cain slowly let Yue-ren's body rest on the bed pulling himself from Yue-ren's spent form and allowing his soft flesh to relax.

He lay on top of Yue-ren both panting with their spent desire and wild passionate dance until he rolled to his side pulling Yue-ren to him, so his head came to rest on his chest.

Yue-ren tried to open his eyes, but his body was exhausted his mind cloudy unfocused as he tried to mouth the words, "thank you" and before fatigue claimed him and he fell into a pure sleep filled with dreams of their love-making as he mouthed, "I love you".

Cain knew that he too was tired, and his body wanted to sleep, but for a moment he watched Yue-ren's sleeping form, the scent of the sweat and sex heavy in the air and the hum of desires and lust becoming a little quieter.

He clasped the sleeping form to him and before he slipped into dreams, ready for them to wake and embrace the world they have been craving he whispered to the night, "I also love you".

Chapter 24

Laphiel

THE MURDEROUS EYE OF THE STORM

WHAT ANGER, WHAT POWERFUL, FREE-FLOWING ANGER that floated in like a mist of glass.

Disgust, true disgust like the smell of corpses in a stagnant pool. These were Laphiel's feelings, his thoughts; he wanted to vomit every inch of his body, his mind his power shivered with loathing and disgust. He had never felt defiled before, never felt so putrid, his skin liked rooting fruit, like the flesh of some long deceased creature.

That vampire had taken what was his, he had touched and tasted something Laphiel had worked so hard to create. He was not only playing with Laphiel's toy, but he was treating it with love, respect and adoration showering it with passions and pleasures giving it all its desires, giving it soul and love. Laphiel was hunched over, holding his stomach as if the worst pain in all his life was ripping into his gut. The floor was dark and dusty, grit beneath his feet crunched as he tried to move about the place he had chosen as a quiet zone.

If he had realised how quickly that vampire was going to heal he would have not been so quick to laugh at him and give him the time he had needed to claim his desire. Laphiel's wounds had almost healed, but in a moment it felt like other beings were tapping into his strength and demonic power, and that feed had weakened him enough to slow down his healing process and allow the unforgivable mistake to be made.

Daylight of the outside world was trying to peer under the door of the mausoleum he was holed up in.

His thought had been that the dead would have brought comfort, and since in this farce of a future people no longer paid much attention to religion, graveyards no longer had protection from creatures of the night. Like many graves in these pretentious cities, they were not blessed and were definitely not sacred instead they were perfect places for demons to come feed off the souls of the newly departed and rest in the darkness and sorrow that always followed the dead.

Humans really had no respect anymore a passing sadness for lost loved ones, then they were left to rot and be forgotten, unaware that their souls had not been adequately cared for and made lovely little snacks for demons needing a leisurely meal or quick fix. This particular tomb was nothing special; a woman, not young really, maybe mid-forties, no children, well none she would admit to or ever saw past their birth just discarding them to their own fates. A pointless death as well, so drunk she had fallen down her own stairs how really stupid, I mean to get that drunk at your party and lose your life by a fall and a snap of the neck.

Maybe that's why Laphiel was in this tomb, at least it was making him smile after all it was a bit of a laugh.

But then the sick feeling washed over him, and all the humour of his little resting spot was gone.

He knew this smell, seen this feeling but only in others.

He had seen it in the lovers of those that he had raped as they looked with disgust at their used and abused partners calling out for forgiveness while feeling dirty. He had smelt the sickness that came when you murdered children, their innocent souls tasting so good while their parents despair soothed you, of course, this was best in the working worlds and human slums when family was all you had, and the pain of losing your own was so much worse than in the big indulgent cities.

But now this feeling, this trembling in the air was more than he had reckoned on, he knew what lust and desire felt like, but this could not be. Cain was making love to his Yue-ren, he wasn't devouring him, taking him, claiming him and torturing him with his own need and wants they were sharing their desire.

Sex could be such a destructive force, sometimes more horrific and painful than violence and yet it was healing all the work Laphiel had put into destroying Yue-ren's soul, and Laphiel knew his beautiful doll was being taken from him completely.

So great was his anger that keeping form had been difficult his face changing to a hundred different faces of people he had seen over the years his body the shape of countless victims.

But now his wounds were healed, and although he hadn't stopped them, he was not going to let them think life was going to be easy for them. To the very end he would fight, this he would kill that perverted excuse for a creature of the night, and with Cain dead, there would be nothing for Yue-ren to hold on to, he would break once more, and Laphiel would have him. Laphiel cleared his thoughts collecting his form and drew himself together creating a tall figure of a man not thin, well sculptured broad-shouldered and muscular arms, his hair short and swept back apart from a few stubborn strands that fell into his face.

His suit was black, underneath you could make out the high collar of a white shirt, but that was the only hint of another colour or item of clothing, his hair naturally was as black as his suite, and his eyes brightest form of green his mind could muster, handsome and confident, these ideas were etched into all his features. Perfect really only a slight annoyance was crossing into his brow as he felt a presence arrive.

"Hello, my dear."

"Going on a date? My you look dashing, I wonder who the lucky person is?"

"Dear little Lillith, I don't have time to play with phantoms. Didn't I warn if you tried to harm Yue-ren there would be consequences, and yes I realised that there was a chance the demon aspect of his blood may awaken, but I didn't think you would make him hate you so much that you would awaken it."

Lillith made a clicking noise with her tongue, trying to bite back the anger she felt, there was no point to arguing now she knew. She'd been created as a distraction but what else did she have left, this monster had created her, and he was the only one she felt any connection with.

"The answer is no, little girl I'm not going to grant you any more of my power. Last time you used it only made my pretty doll angry and strong, and that's not my wish. Oh and no I won't end it either, you see, I'd like to say you are nothing no me and I couldn't care less about your existence, but unfortunately for both of us, I have a reason to acknowledge you. You awoke Yue-ren, you gave him the strength to fight back, and therefore I feel the need to punish you. You will stay as you are a ghost, so don't look at me with sadness. Did you think a demon would show compassion?"

"Then allow me this favour, if I am destined to exist if I must be a phantom, let me watch. I wanna be the witness to the final duel. I want to see who wins I want to be the one that sees Cain die so I can keep the story forever as my legacy. To tell it to those that might listen, when they ask what happened in this city, why so many were killed and why it is so haunted, I want to be there to whisper the tale into the night. This story will be mine, and therefore I won't die or disappear as I will be remembered as the one that knows the truth behind this city and that monster who roamed the night and preyed on humans. That desire can be deadly and powerful."

"A story keeper, well so be it; once Cain is dead, and Yue-ren is mine I will have no need for this city so I suppose you can have it, after all, a ghost needs a good place to haunt. Well if we're quite finished, I have battled to fight and a prize to win."

With that the doors of the tomb spread open, the midday sun shone in bathing the dark figure with all its glory as he stepped out into the world.

The day was half gone, but he had the advantage, even six hours of sunshine was enough to stop that vampire he was going to win this. With confidence, he stood into the world, through the sun-drenched graveyard with all its angels looking sad and lonely in their stone prisons. Into the street, he walked past ladies with sun umbrellas talking on corners, before stopping to look at the handsome gentleman that strode by and trying to ignore the cold chill of something else passing by they couldn't see.

Even at this time the world was quiet, a few people off for shopping or lunch in the plazas and markets places, little cafes smelling of expensive coffee and handmade cakes. All so stupid to Laphiel, indulgent children it really was an entire city of selfish small children that knew nothing of the world they inhabited. The occasional carriage drove by, sunlight glinting off its polished metal and glass windows. If he had been more human, he would have thought how beautiful a day it was, so still and fresh, warm and comforting but these ideas were thus lost to him. No, Laphiel was following a much more dirty fragrance, lust, need, want and desire, the smell of sex and passion, thick and heavy.

Hot blood, its light sent on the air, he knew he was nearer them, those disgusting creatures.

He had turned the corner another street like so many but one building that seemed darker and more imposing than the rest. The tree in front did not blossom like all the others that framed the street. All the windows were shut, and it looked like they had never been opened. The small front garden unattended, a few bushes and brambles, their thorns twisting into the iron gate.

The doorway, dense wood with delicate designs of swirling patterns carved into it and the handle a cast iron rose, its petals slightly pulled back.

"Well," thought Laphiel. "He really should knock first."

He placed his hand on the doorknob and watched as the iron melted and turned red glowing and hot while the molten drops fell onto the floor and door caused black smoke to rise and little sparks from the internal electrics fizzled into the air as if soldered away. The door itself began to quiver, little flames starting to lick the surface running up the frame until there was an archway of fire.

Thick black smoke was all ready to rise up, and a meter diameter area where Laphiel stood was beginning to melt, the air hot causing a mirage water effect where he stood. Soon people were beginning to look out of their homes, and a few started to gather in the street transfixed by the dancing flames and the man at the centre. In a second, an explosion had been set off Laphiel had been engulfed in his flames, and a crater was all that could be seen where the front of the house had been.

Nearly all the houses in the street had had their windows blown out, and the viewers in the road had been knocked back by the hot wave that had spread out.

All witnesses to the explosion now lay unconscious, their bodies scattered around the street while the house began to burn brilliantly.

There was no debris from the front section of the house; instead, heavy rain of ash began to fall. The flames had spread beginning to engulf the homes on each side. But not this house, something was stopping the rest of the house from setting ablaze.

Laphiel stepped into the burnt wreckage and looked up into a dark and hidden corner. Amber eyes stared back at him from the shadow as Cain hid his body from the sun that was trying to break into his home. Laphiel smiled, collected the flames into a burning ball and let it explode out with savage ferocity. It was like a dragon gone berserk, feeding on blind rage, trying to engulf all in its path.

The flames licked every inch, they could be found spiralling around every surface until an area of about a mile in diameter was ablaze. It looked like a war zone, surfaces scorched and blackened, bodies burnt beyond recognition and think heavy black smoke rising into the air. All around choking ash fell to the ground, darkening it like tainted snow.

The very souls of those not so innocent beings denied rising to the heavens, instead falling back to earth as this impure dirty rain stained and tainted.

Yet this small section of the house, nothing more than a

room now suspended in this zone of devastation. With the sun behind it, the roof cast enough shadow to protect the figure within from its harmful rays.

Laphiel made an annoyed noise sucking air in through his teeth and trying not to let his annoyance show on his face. Damn that vampire he had enough power to form a barrier. And as amber eyes looked out the flames could be seen dancing in the reflection. But that was not all, the fire also illuminated a part of the room before hidden, a light orange glow reflecting off the whiteness in the blackness.

Yue-ren was standing just to the left of Cain, a sheet hiding his body as his hair looked slightly damp and tousled, thin strands stuck to the sweat of his brow. Amongst the flames and the ash-framed by pillars of dark smoke he never seemed so pure, like a dove in a flock of ravens or a lily in a valley of thorn roses he stood pure and brilliant. If he had been shocked by what had happened, he didn't show it. His face was calm and focused, he was concentrating.

Yue-ren walked to Cain's side and then that hateful vampire took a step forward, a step into the light and smiled.

His skin did not burn, he did not move to protect himself from the remaining light he looked as calm and confident as Laphiel himself had felt.

Laphiel knew what this meant, it was not his flames that made Yue-ren glow it was his own power, he was shielding Cain. As soon as this knowledge hit him so did Cain's first attack. A hail of deadly ice was raining at him, quenching the flames around Laphiel's body and turning up more thick black smoke. Laphiel jumped into the air, and in an instant, Cain was in front of him, Laphiel blocked the first and second blow, Cain's hand ripping across his shirt and

Laphiel thrust his own hand forward scratching along the cheekbone of Cain's face.

New flames swam towards him forming a hot molten ball that fired at Cain. Cain stretched his arm out, a wall of ice shielding him, hot steam hissing into the air and causing warm droplets to fall to the ground. The remaining ice wall reformed into a javelin and flew at Laphiel only to be caught in a mass of black chains and shattered into icy shards.

The chains whipped round destroying anything in their path before targeting the vampire before them.

The rest of the scene had continued to burn but now so much smoke, and ash had been thrown up it had formed a thick cloud, polluting the air and blocking out the sun's rays.

This was Cain's opportunity, he nodded to Yue-ren who dropped his protective shield as both knew that Yue-ren could not have kept it up the whole fight and it was preventing Cain from using all his abilities. Just as the chains were about to capture their prize, they broke into a formless shadow, and this shadow began to fracture into a mass of bats. They screeched and flew surrounding Laphiel in a cloud of fangs and teeth. But Laphiel knew this trick, and he started to warm up the air around him causing the creatures to grow hot and weak until they dropped to the floor and Cain had regained his shape.

The warm vortex swam round Laphiel, its superheated barrier preventing Cain from getting physically close to him. Instead, Cain called forth large ice spikes breaking through the ground up to the monster in the sky. Laphiel danced round them hissing when one got a little too close and ripped his clothes, he tried to get higher but saw a twinkle of light as a hail of icy javelins rained down on him.

It was too late, they tore into him pinning him to the

ground, impaling him through every limb as he tried to rip his body from the restraining spires.

Laphiel was not defeated yet, as he looked to the sky above him, ash rain settling on his face his dark blood mixing on the floor creating thick dirty pools as the spires began to melt until he was lying in a horrid pool of water, ash, blood and dirt.

As Cain approached him the pool began to bubble, the water warmed till it was a hot sludge that fired itself at Cain. Even with his arms to block the putrid tar, it clung to him burning into his flesh.

Laphiel was no longer watching, he was gathering his fire, his essence of hell, he knew around him that was what the scene must look like, that he was back in the belly of his home wishing so much that he was up in the human world searching for far better ways to enjoy himself. Even with hell all around him, the smell of burning flesh and the wounded he wanted to see the light, not hear the roars of flames or screams of those in pain or being tortured, he wanted to be in a world where he created his own pain and torture. In that instant, his world became even more heated and warm, a column of pure brilliant blue flame. It was strong, pushing Cain back from where he stood; even Yue-ren could feel the heat, raising an arm to shield his eyes from the light.

The column exploded up into the sky clearing all in its path piercing, smoke, ash and cloud and allowing the sun to shine down.

It was getting closer to evening, but the light was still warm and healthy, it had been such a shock, Yue-ren hadn't conceded what it meant, and he had been too late to put up the barrier. Cain's flesh began to burn not as fast or vigorously as midday sun but even this evening glow hurt. He screamed, trying to retreat back, into a safe shadow trying to get out of direct sunlight before the pain and burning took over his senses.

Yue-ren panicked, he had not acted fast enough, and now Cain was in pain. Yue-ren had to move quickly, had to do something as he jumped from his perch above the wreckage of Cain's home. Laphiel smiled, pulling himself off the floor. He barely kept his human appearance or form, instead appearing as if a man had melted into tar, black and thick. His eyes were red now, and he had no hair as all his skin was black, what remained of one arm was outstretched dripping its form onto the floor as his legs looked more like the roots of trees trying to break free from the ground.

The chains gathered around him, and a smile played on what was left of a mouth losing form. The chains sprang forward, ready to pierce the creature before them, to spear right through it and end it all.

Laphiel could feel his body freezing, turning to ice before all was black, it was all over; coldness, then darkness, then there was nothing.

Lillith smiled, she felt her weakness as she watched Laphiel disappear, his body freeze then fracture each shard eaten away by a white glow, and she had witnessed the end.

Now in the soot and ash filled shadow, this moment was all that was left, the sun was again hidden by smoke, but it didn't matter it was setting anyway she had seen the end. Laphiel looked on, blood on snow was what it looked like, and he had always loved how beautiful that image was, the crimson of blood so much more powerful when on the pureness of snow.

That was his last image as cold rushed over him, chains fell slack and disappeared into a faint winter glow reflected off the inky blackness of his skin as he felt he could no longer move, then a dagger of ice to seal his fate till he fell out of existence.

Chapter 25

Yue-ren

AND THE CURTAIN FALLS

Yue-ren had never felt so satisfied, so full, so raw, so passionate.

All his senses had been alive, and now he felt warm and content in Cain's embrace.

How many times had they made love that night, how many times had he called out Cain's name in pure rapturous delight?

His body was sated, he felt damp in all the places Cain had touched him, and he blushed deeply.

Yue-ren had been the first to drift off to sleep, and the first to awaken knowing it must be day outside, and the vampire would probably sleep all day.

Even in sleep, Cain looked powerful, his muscular body holding Yue-ren to him, his hair cascading all over the pillow like golden snakes keeping a watchful eye out on both the forms they looked over. Yue-ren's own hair was messy and tousled with damp strands clinging to his face, he felt like spring all the coldness and ice of his life melting into the warm embrace he was wrapped in. He would have laughed at the idea feeling the warmth from a vampire, a creature of death giving him life and yet it all made sense.

He wasn't human so why worry about human concerns it didn't matter what they were as long as they had each other and the delicious heat they created.

His lips felt swollen and sore, a slight sting from the cut on his thigh and he knew there would be dark bruises looking more violent against his skin where Cain had held him. But the aches and scathes were all worth it, for the feeling of being filled and pleasured still clung to him, made his body tremble a little at the memory.

No, nothing in this world mattered any more, he didn't care about anything but Cain and their life together, no ghost girls or jealous demons would tear them apart.

So what if said demon had made some shocking revelations, it didn't matter what was in his blood, the world hadn't accepted him, but Cain had, so if he was less human than it didn't matter as his lover wasn't human at all. In fact, having a demon in him meant he had even less regret for throwing away his human life and giving everything to this creature of the night. He had embraced all of what he was because it all belonged to Cain and Cain had accepted all of it.

Yue-ren was able to cast aside human frailty, intolerance, insecurity and weakness to embrace this dark side of life where there was nothing but his passions and desires. For the first time he felt strong: as the blush rose in his cheeks, he felt passionate.

He was more than awake now and so very close to Cain that he could taste the vampire skin.

He opened his mouth allowing his tongue to flicker across the skin of the vampire, it tasted dark even Cain's sweat tasted like midnight and power but most of all desire. The taste intoxicated him, and he wished the vampire would wake. Yue-ren hoped that Cain would turn him so that they could be like this for always, so they could make love all night and sleep all day, he thought of the idea of feeding together, of sharing warm blood until their stomachs were full and other desires needed to be sated.

He also wondered what his demon side would do once turned. Would he grow stronger, the more he embraced this new life and cast away his human life the more power he felt within him?

But now all he wanted was for amber eyes to stare down at him. As he looked up he saw Cain stir, amber eyes indeed opening and then the snapped into full recognition. But it wasn't going to play out the way Yue-ren hoped, those eyes weren't looking at him, they stared off beyond him at some unknown invader trying to break into their moment.

Just as Cain knew Yue-ren also got a feeling, a feeling that told him, "He's coming".

Cain's words were dark angry but composed as he slipped from the bed, Yue-ren feeling cold and empty.

In an instant, Cain's clothes seem to melt onto him, and he turned to his lover now sitting up on the bed. The sheet had fallen to Yue-ren's lap hiding him from Cain's eye, but exposed was a darkly bruised hip bone and a pure white canvas marked with red flecks, the proof of their night's desires.

Yue-ren's eyes were slightly misty but regaining focus and understanding and his damp hair clung to his face while the rest looked wild and windswept from their own desire and lusts. Yue-ren knew who was coming; he could feel it in his blood and at the same time he felt warm like a fire of anger was growing in the pit of his stomach. Not now was all he could think; he wasn't going to let that creature destroy this. He was happy he had found what he had been looking for and be damned who stood in their way and disrupted his newfound passion. Yue-ren wrapped the sheet around his form, some of it clinging to the little damp parts of his body as he stood on the other side of the bed, both men anticipating the coming of this storm.

It had been such a blur, such a torrent of flame, darkness, light, power and anger.

The sound had been horrifying, far worse than the heat and brightness of the flames. Yue-ren hadn't even really thought, all he knew was his world was ripped apart for the world as a whole to witness. He had thought how crisp the daylight was and how burnt the ground was and then the horrifying thought that this light could burn his beloved.

It had been in that instance the barrier had come up shielding them both from the light outside and buying them time for the ash to block out the suns invasion and give Cain the chance he needed. Watching the battle had been difficult at first trying to concentrate on Cain's safety and then giving the vampire his freedom.

The two enemies had moved fast, sometimes too quickly for Yue-ren's eyes to catch and with so many images flashing before him. It was a war, not just the destroyed area around them but between these two creatures of darkness and power. It was a war of fire and ice, light and dark, a battle for revenge, for hatred, for lust and desires all the things a war shouldn't be fought for. It was a war for Yue-ren, a man the world had never fought for only imprisoned, but this world of vampires, demons and creatures the human world denied was fighting over him, and he knew he was destined to be part of this, this was his war.

It was when it looked like Cain was going to be the victor that the great beam of light had ripped through the soot and ash. It had torn a hole in the world and let in the cursed sun and its vengeful light causing Yue-ren to shield his eyes.

When he heard Cain's scream he knew he was too late, the sun had begun to burn, and Yue-ren could feel tears in his eyes. He had lost his voice, or maybe it was just sound that had fallen in this void. Yue-ren's world was spinning, he couldn't feel the floor beneath him, but the rushing sensation of wind meant he was definitely in motion. His single thought was Cain, and then pain and shadow.

The sun retreated, and the ash and soot floated around like snow falling. Laphiel looked confused, and if possible sad, if the demon had more of his features Yue-ren would have been sure that sadness had crept over the demon's face.

He felt the bolt of cold rush past him and saw the arrow of ice pierce the creature in front before the demon seemed to crack and break off into none existence.

His belly felt warm, wet and sticky, but the rest of him was feeling cold. His arms, which had been out at either side of him lost their strength and fell to his side, and he looked down.

His vision was getting blurry, and he was aware of a great pain which all of a sudden increased to unbearable as he heard what sounded like chains falling to the ground. He looked down and saw the wound in his stomach, brought his hands up to hold the chains that were embedded there, letting his blood flow down his naked body.

The sheet he had worn was long discarded, probably carried off in the wind of the storm and he was there standing naked in a battlefield of raining ash, the world growing quiet and dark. The chains faded which only meant his blood flowed faster, and then the world slanted, he was falling backwards.

So slow; it was so slow, he could feel his hair flutter in

front of him, warm blood running down his frame and the sensation that the floor was beyond his reach and he would fall forever.

It was cold, it was lonely, and it was frightening.

Strong arms caught him in an embrace he knew well, the scent so familiar, he could hear a voice he knew well calling his name as he tried to focus on the tiny glimpse of amber he could see; before him.

Yue-ren raised an arm; his hand was caught in a warm grip as fingers laced with his own. His other hand had lifted to find a face, his finger lightly gliding over the features trying to work out why his sensations were dulling. He felt soft, wet drops on his face, they were not rain, and his eyes had become dry.

Was Cain crying? Why would the vampire need to shed tears?

"Cain, Cain what, what's happening?"

His own voice scared him, it was light and hoarse not at all confident but what scared him more was that he could hear the fear in Cain's or a note of panic.

When Cain spoke next, the confidence and composure had been regained while Yue-ren was even more confused. Even wrapped in Cain's embrace he felt cold, and why could he not see? Why it was all so black?

"Its time Yue-ren, its time for you to join me. We'll be creatures of the night, just let it wash over you and when you awake we will be inseparable".

Cain's words felt so comforting and so exciting to Yue-ren. Yue-ren felt Cain's hot breath on his neck, it seemed so much more intense compared to the coldness of the rest of his body.

Then teeth, two like needles piercing his flesh, breaking the skin followed by warm lips. The pain was gone as quickly as it came; instead, Yue-ren could only feel Cain's darkest and most potent of kisses.

Yue-ren's head was light and spinning, there was nearly no feeling in him, no sensations only the heat at his neck and then it was gone. Cain drew back then using a nail cut a line across his wrist and put it to Yue-ren's lips.

"Drink."

It was neither a command nor a suggestion, it was an offer, and Yue-ren knew this, he tried to move his lips, could just about taste warm, precious blood.

First, just a drop, more intoxicating than Cain's sweat had been. It tasted of the night but more it felt like life and death, it tasted like a thousand hot and passionate midnights, the kind of night decadent humans had tried so long to create but failed. This one drop of blood was like tasting the boundaries of heaven and hell, a forbidden world to humans. Yue-ren wanted more; in his darkness, in this cold, he wanted this blood.

The hand that has been stroking Cain's face fell to his side, the other lost its grip, only Cain was holding the delicate fingers resting in his own.

A cry rang out that would have been enough to wake the dead; it would be a sound that would haunt the living for all their lives.

It was wild, untamed, it was violent, and it was from a pit of despair no human would ever understand. Cain's howl rang out into the early darkness screaming like a madman, like the very forces of hell had been unleashed on him and were trying to rip his body and soul apart.

It had been too late; Cain pulled the body in his arms even closer to him as if trying to force them together. The sky had begun to clear, the stars of the night sky visible, but Cain did not move. It was grief beyond mortal understanding, and like a madman, he had lost all thought and reason apart from cradling the still form in his arms.

This had been why he hadn't seen them arrive; if he had been alert, or even if he had thought it through, it wouldn't have been hard to work out what would happen next.

Giant explosions, fire, smoke and a pavement littered with corpses were not something you could hide or ignore. Even the first of the city's so-called police knew whatever was happening in the cloud of ash was beyond them, so while they waited for it to clear a more powerful military force had begun to converge. Even in such decadent and selfish times, there was still the need for some military power a force to be called in just in case.

Of course, this force usually came to disrupt riots in the poverty-stricken cities, or dissatisfied working classes trying to rebel against the more affluent towns of the aris-tocracy. After the many wars that had plagued the world people no longer really cared that much for fighting, not when increased wealth meant you could indulge in things and didn't need to fight for anything. The only ones that resisted were the poor and unwanted, and they never put up much of a battle. So now most weapons of any real damage had been lost in ancient battles, and the military hadn't really evolved much in recent years.

Guns and bullets had always been enough to stop rioting working classes as they couldn't even afford the luxury of a handgun.

And now, here they were, the uninvolved gun wielding military about to face what they could only describe as a monster.

Cain didn't even look up or move as he heard the click of weapons, or the heavy footfall of soldiers as they approached him, he really couldn't care less about the little dots of red that targeted him and marked him.

No, it was when they called out to him, and he would have ignored them if not for the stupid request they made.

"Put the woman down and move away."

What a stupid thing to say, what an insult, what a mistake.

"Put HIM down, who the hell are you to ask that of me? You have no idea what I am, you have no idea who the boy is within my arms, and yet you tell me to put him down. If you even had the slightest clue, you would know that this delicate beauty is male and not female, but alas you are stupid and undeserving. I will do no such thing now move away."

"I repeat put the… boy…"

"I WILL NEVER PUT HIM DOWN!"

Everything shuddered; the ground trembled and vibrated like a small earthquake and yet there was a deadly silence in the air, tenseness and quietness.

Cain stood, eyes of amber slowly turning red, blood pumping hard in his veins. The first gunshot caught him in the forehead, a clear, perfect shot that caused his neck to bend back and Cain to step back. His body was curved back slightly, but Yue-ren was still tight in his grip as he brought his body forward and straightened his stance.

The bullet worked its way back out of the wound, as the little trail of blood flowed from the round mark on his head and dripped off his chin. Cain smiled he could see the look of confusion and fear on each face around them, he could smell the fear, it made him excited. The little hole in his temple healed and he smiled as he began to walk toward the soldier that had shot him.

In a flash it was over; at his feet lay the soldier, his head, a meter from the body and a wave of blood tears had rained on those standing closest to him.

He heard the command to fire as those behind him took

aim and a flock of bullets flew at him. How cowardly, he thought, to shoot a man in the back as he turned to meet the hail that was heading for him. As they reached, each bullet missed and then fell to the ground in its own little tomb of ice. But the wave of cold didn't stop there; no it continued on until each man stood frozen a look of pure terror on their faces.

Then all hell broke loose.

A hail of bullets, metal rained at him as Cain jumped through the ice sculptures before him. The bullets tore through each ice figure shattering them and embedding bullets into everything apart from the one thing they were meant for. Cain leapt up, and before all a cloud, a living moving swirling cloud formed, part breaking off to shield and carry the still form of Yue-ren, the other a screeching mass that dove forward as fast and deadly as any swarm of bullets. The bats attacked tearing at anyone they could, ripping and biting.

The screams could be heard down the street, all the way to the still blazing houses.

The fires had continued to spread, and no matter what the flames were fought with they continued to burn. It was like hell itself had summoned them, and they were devouring everything in their path. What else could the military do but call in more troops and firefighters?

The next wave threw gas cans which meant the bats had to retreat out into a safe distance. Cain regained form in the street in front of the line of defence that had now secured its location. Yue-ren was still clutched to his breast, and his face was a mask of pure rage and anger.

"This place, this city, you all did this, you are all to blame. You took something beautiful and destroyed it; you took everything for granted, never trying to think of what your world was doing to those different from it. You all make me sick, you will all pay."

Even as Cain spoke a new hail was thrown at him, this time grenades which only made Cain laugh.

The first couple of grenades were met by a wall of ice, simply exploding and causing shards of vicious, cold metal and ice fragments to rain down. Others just stopped in mid-air and then faster than any human could throw, they rained in all directions bringing destruction in their wake. Before anyone could retaliate the road trembled and split, as pillars of ice ripped out from the ground destroying the entire street, not stopping till they had ripped their way through half of the city before them.

Those not killed by the icy spears looked on in horror, as ice skewered teammates and civilians alike. Cain ran forward, his free hand ripped its way through anyone in his path. The screams were horrific, the dying sounds of maybe a hundred men, as he reached the centre of the city, a sea of corpses and blood filling the street.

Cain was not done yet, he was only beginning.

Every corpse on the floor rolled over, each one with a grenade gave up the small weapon. Cain smiled as the sound of one hundred pins falling to the ground rippled in the night followed by the great chorus of a hundred explosions in a hundred different scattered directions. People were beginning to flee, to run from their location to run for their lives before flames or ice engulfed them.

But Cain was quicker, and he began to lose count as bodies fell to the floor, some ripped in half, others with bleeding wounds from the impact of Cain's hand. Cain himself was drenched in blood, it stained his clothes, his hair, it was spattered across his face, and it was painted on the body still cradled in his arm. He paused a moment to look at his love, silent cold and delicate. Cain wiped the blood that was freckling Yue-ren's pale face leaving little red smudges.

His skin was so cold and soft, his features reflecting the incandescent light of a city engulfed by flames. Even now he was the most beautiful creature Cain had yet seen, Yue-ren was the most precious of loves, and the world would pay for robbing him of that.

As Cain walked, behind him spires of ice crashed out from the shadow of each, and in front, a collection of abandoned carriages littered the road.

Cain concentrated, and the vehicles hovered off the ground, then were crashed into the surrounding houses causing a new chorus of an explosion to erupt. What a beautiful symphony he was creating, a musical masterpiece the very song of destruction. Those in the houses that had not been killed instantly were trying to pull their broken and torn bodies from the wreckage only to face a pair of red eyes and a flash of cold vengeance.

By now the entire city was ablaze and whatever military force that was left tried to gather at the remaining undestroyed area. Their last stand against this rampaging monster that they believed had no right to exist in this world. All those civilians not destroyed and killed were trying to evacuate to this area, no longer worrying about their possessions, just trying to get out alive.

They ran like a flood of wild and frightened children seeking salvation.

Cain had taken to the rooftops, not a building behind him was left untouched, and behind him, it looked like pure Armageddon.

This city had been hell to Yue-ren, and now it was just that to every human in it. The sound of the dying and frightened, the smell of burning, death, spilt blood and chaos, it all served them right. Cain looked down, nothing but contempt on his face, the last of the inhabitants of this disgusting town running down a street they thought would lead to salvation. Well, he would be the judge of that, in fact, he would be this city's judge, jury and executioner.

Every window shivered and then broke, a thousand windows all breaking at once, this was like a giant cymbal being rung out in the middle of Cain's symphony. The glass cut through all and another chorus of screaming erupted signifying it was nearly the end. In fact, this whole night had been like going to the opera, there was the beginning, middle and now the passionate but tragic ending. This opera had seen the sad death of a hero and the wrath of the one sworn to avenge this death.

Yes, this was Cain and Yue-ren's opera, the last verse of dying screams and then the finale.

Cain descended into the chaos, looked at his orchestra and gave a bow, he then lifted his arm and began to conduct.

First was the rattle of fear, of trembling guns trying to keep a grip on their weapons, then the little crackles of the fire punctuated with a few larger bangs as these flames caused something to explode once hot enough. Then that tiny and delicate tingle of pins dropping to the floor once again, before the great cymbal crash of grenade explosions.

The chorus of screams and the bang of drums as bodies thrown from the blast hit walls and streets and parked vehicles. Then there was a great crash, and from behind the chaos where people were trying to escape the town a giant wall of ice expelled itself up into the air. How is a conductor meant to finish his opera if the orchestra runs away?

Cain raised his arm in the air, and a strange silence fell over the chaos. Nearly everyone was dead or beyond help even those dying or in great pain kept still, and quiet and those left unharmed just stood, rooted by fear and the strange silence that hung over them. Cain smiled and dropped his arm signifying the final chord of his master-piece. The ice wall was rumbling and shaking, it cracked and chipped and then came down.

A wall of dense, dark ice descended, crushing every-thing below it.

Some had enough to scream but most didn't, silenced forever by this opera of death and destruction. Some ice fell into the flames causing loud hissing sounds as hot and cold collided and steam rose into the air. The air was warm and damp, it was heavy with a thousand burnt fragrances, death clinging to it, blanketing the city in midnight hell on earth.

And as chaos ruled and swarmed Cain cleared his mind and focused on what he had created.

Cain began to walk forward, and then he felt a familiar presence behind him, eyes of loathing and disgust trying to penetrate him.

"Why, tell me this why, why am I still here?"

"You don't listen do you girl. You really don't, I told you, you are connected to that demon's blood only by destroying its blood will you be freed from this ghostly curse."

"But I saw him killed, Yue-ren took your final blow and was killed, Laphiel is dead."

"His blood hasn't been completely destroyed; after all, you've seen, how do you not understand how darkness works?"

"Yue-ren, it's him, the demon's blood is in him."

"And in me, as I have tasted Yue-ren's blood. Yue-ren may not have drunk my blood but like all demons, he still exists, you are proof of that."

Lillith looked at the vampire before her, she was confused, her anger blinding her from any truth or under-standing.

She had seen Laphiel die, she had seen Yue-ren die so why, why the hell was she not free?

Cain saw the confusion, he didn't have the patience for this but felt since he was partly responsible for her fate, and he would give her one last piece of truth.

"Laphiel is dead, his body destroyed; his essence, his demonic soul, is back in hell where it will stay without a body, trapped there. Yue-ren is dead, but his body is not destroyed, a part of him lives with me, and as for his soul it is somewhere out in the world, for it is tied to mine now."

"So what vampire? You are going to wander the world looking for your lover's lost soul and reunite it? Well then, since my body is dead, but my spirit seems to exist in this world, I have no choice but to follow you. If you find a way to return the soul to the body, I'm sure there must be a way to return my spirit to a new body. It looks like you have a travelling companion, my dear Cain."

Cain only barely noticed her words, as he began to walk, he stepped away from the chaos and the city behind him into the night leaving the cursed landscape, not even turning back to face frustrated screams when they came.

"NO, NO, NOOOO! WHY WHY THE HELL NOT!"

Cain sighed and still not looking back spoke.

"A ghost is tied to the place they died, they cannot leave it."

Lillith looked on, shocked, as the figure of the vampire walked into the darkness leaving her behind. She couldn't move, invisible forces keeping her trapped. Cain walked on, the last thing he heard being Lilith's threats screamed at him.

"I won't stay tied forever, vampire. I may be a ghost, but I was created by a demon. I will find a way, I will! You have left me in a city full of ghosts, thousands of spirits all hating you for causing their deaths. I will use their anger, devour each lost soul, I'm the queen of the dead here and I'll find a way, I will escape and chase you down this is not the end, not the end!"

But even as she screamed Cain was already flitting into the night and Lillith was left in her city of ghosts, her own private hell, with no idea how to keep any of her threats.

Cain rushed through the night his body was dirty, stained with the blood of so many victims their blood turned dark and crusted over his clothes and hair.

One hand so soaked in blood he wondered if it would ever wash off. He felt a feeling in his stomach, so angry had he been he had forgotten to feed, and he was feeling empty. But it wasn't just the lack of a meal that left him vacant, it was the cold body in his arms. Even like this Yue-ren was beautiful, and in the unrestricted glow of moonlight, it looked like his body shone.

Yue-ren's skin reflected each glow of moonlight bathing both men in its eerie glow until they looked like spectres flying through the night. Cain would find a way; like all endings, it was really only a beginning. He had lived so very long, he had forgotten all about time, it was not a concept he cared much for. He had so much time to spare it didn't matter how much he used because one-day Yue-ren would wake and they would be able to spend the rest of their eternity together.

He had waited this long to find such a beautiful creature, what was a little more time now? The wind rushed past them, silence filled the air, and all the sounds of the city died out in this last crescendo, signifying the end, as he looked down on the form in his arms, amber eyes intense and focused.

"It is done ,Yue-ren - our legacy, our opera. But now it is time to find a new stage and a new song."

About the Author

Zoe Burgess is an upcoming author inspired by the works she has read and the genres she loves.

Zoe spent her university years studying Media, Japanese Creative Industries and holds two Masters in this field, specialising in Gender and Sexuality in anime. This lead to expanding her love of manga and anime, presenting research at conventions and conferences, as well as setting up her own art business. The stories and worlds discovered during this time was what inspired her own writing.

Zoe realised that her passion for fantasy, her imagination and desire for non heteronormative story telling could be explored in the fictional worlds she creates.

Now she writes the stories that she herself would love to read and explores themes and genres close to her heart.